P9-BBQ-650

THE FALL

JAMES PRELLER

Feiwel and Friends

New York

A Feiwel and Friends Book
An Imprint of Macmillan

 Printed in the United States of America by R. R. Donnelley & Sons Company, Harrisonburg, Virginia. For information, address Feiwel and Friends, 175 Fifth Avenue, New York, N.Y. 10010.

Feiwel and Friends books may be purchased for business or promotional use. For information on bulk purchases, please contact the Macmillan Corporate and Premium Sales Department at (800) 221-7945 x5442 or by e-mail at specialmarkets@macmillan.com.

Library of Congress Cataloging-in-Publication Data

Preller, James.
The fall / James Preller. — First edition.
pages cm

Summary: In writing in his journal about middle-school classmate Morgan Mallen's suicide from bullying, Sam explores whether he was a friend, or one of the bullies who ignored her at school and tormented her online.

ISBN 978-0-312-64301-0 (hardback) — ISBN 978-1-250-06647-3 (e-book)
[1. Self-actualization (Psychology)—Fiction. 2. Suicide—Fiction. 3. Bullies—Fiction. 4. Cyberbullying—Fiction. 5. Diaries—Fiction.] I. Title.
PZ7.P915Fal 2015
[Fic]—dc23
2015002566

Book design by Ashley Halsey

Feiwel and Friends logo designed by Filomena Tuosto

First Edition: 2015

10 9 8 7 6 5 4 3 2 1

mackids.com

This book is dedicated to my mother

Special thanks to Mark Lane, who read and responded to the original manuscript

I've come to understand and to believe that each of us is more than the worst thing we've ever done.

—Bryan Stevenson, TED Talks, March 5, 2012

I wonder if I've been changed in the night? Let me think. Was I the same when I got up this morning? I almost think I can remember feeling a little different. But if I'm not the same, the next question is "Who in the world am I?" Ah, that's the great puzzle!

—Lewis Carroll, *Alice in Wonderland*

NOT LIKE ME

Two weeks before Morgan Mallen threw herself off the water tower, I might have typed a message on her social media page that said, "Just die! Die! Die! No one cares about you anyway!"

(I'm just saying, it could have been me.)

And I say "could have" because the message was anonymous. Untraceable. Nobody knows who said that horrible thing. That was the beauty of the deal. Nobody knew exactly who said what, except for Athena, I guess. The rest of us sent messages from the shadow places and let them run loose like wolves in the forest.

No one was responsible.

I sure don't know who typed what. Whose fingers punched the keys? Who said such cruel, unspeakable things? I wonder, *Could it have been me*?

No, that wasn't like me at all.

CAST OUT

I barely knew her. Not many people did. But I knew this: She was out there.

Ladies and gentlemen of the jury, I ask you: Am I not allowed to say even that? It doesn't make me a bad person for stating the obvious. It was a fact—Morgan Mallen was different, but not in a good way. Like in a *waaaaay* way.

For example: The sky is gray, the grass is green, and Morgan Mallen became the saddest girl I'd ever seen. It even rhymes. Green, seen, mean, teen, sardine.

(Etcetera, etcetera.)

Some girls in school claimed she was this and alleged she was that. There was also a selfie that famously made the rounds. She maybe kissed the wrong boy. Who knows what really happened.

Once a message was spray-painted on the girls' bathroom door, and another day it appeared on the side of the snack shack by the football field: "Morgan Mallen is a slut."

Check that tense. *Was*, not *is*.

Was a tramp. A selfie-sharer. An outcast.

None of this makes me a bad person.

Right?

SLOGANS ON SHIRTS

There are a lot of phonies in this town, I'll tell you that much.

A lot of them.

(A lot.)

The whole anti-bullying campaign is suddenly everywhere. Posters in the hallways, words on everybody's lips during morning announcements, in classrooms.

Somebody made a big sign for the front of the school:

THIS IS A BULLY-FREE ZONE!

So, *whew*, that's a relief. Now we can feel good about ourselves again. We forgive everybody, even the creeps. Please admire our cleaned-up images, like shiny pennies in a sock drawer—and about as useful.

The whole town was at the funeral, stunned and sobbing.

Long-sleeved T-shirts were handed out for the students to wear, announcing to the world that we were SOLDIERS AGAINST BULLYING! We didn't even have to buy the shirts. Just pulled them over our heads, like wool over somebody's eyes. Now look at us, TV cameras: We're good peeps. *Baa!*

Do unto others. Yeah, right, we've memorized all the best slogans.

But at night we peel off our shirts. We stand barefoot and alone before the bathroom mirror, examining ourselves through hollow eyes. And we know. Deep down we know what we did and didn't do.

I sometimes wonder how Morgan would have reacted. You know that bracelet some people wear, WWJD? Jesus, I honestly don't know. I think about Morgan, if she could look down on us from some fluffy cloud in outer space or wherever. I think she'd laugh out loud—an empty, sad, sarcastic laugh. The way she usually laughed, a little crookedly. She'd look at all of us wearing shirts like Halloween costumes. Masking our true selves. She might even be looking down on us right now, laughing at the big joke. *Ho-ho-ho.*

Funniest thing ever.

ONE SPECTACULAR FACT

Don't expect to get all the facts from me. Okay? She stepped off the water tower. A spectacular statement, concise and final. That's the only fact you're going to need. Says it all right there.

So don't get the idea this journal will be some kind of complete document where you learn "her story," or even "my story."

There are holes in this leaky ship. We could all drown together.

All the cops standing around like on detective shows, scratching their heads, saying, "There are things here we still don't know."

No kidding.

I do have impressions, details, memories. I'll write down some things that happened. Try to remember.

Maybe it will help.

I will sit down, open this book to a clean page, and set the timer on my cell to fifteen minutes. That's the promise I've made to myself. Or maybe it's the promise I've made to her. The least I can give. If time's up, that's that. Even if the page stays blank.

THE GAME

A lot of people wrote a ton of trash. You want specifics? It became this thing we all did sometime last year, around the start of school. It was a game of tag, basically. And what's a game without rules? That was Athena's idea. She devised the system, set the guidelines, enforced the rules.

No comment could be longer than twenty-five words. And it was important, very important, that every comment was anonymous, like a Secret Santa, but, you know, way different. The opposite of a gift.

There was a bright-blue piece of laminated poster board, about half the size of an index card. In red letters it said:

TAG. YOUR TURN.

Another rule: You had twenty-four hours to post the next message. That was important too. You had to keep it going, you know, and not think about it too much.

(That was the trick, the "not thinking.")

When it was your turn, you had to post a secret comment

on Morgan Mallen's stupid page, then you slipped the note back into Athena Luikin's locker, and she tagged somebody else. "You're it." That was how she controlled the game. If you didn't go along, you were *out*. Not out of the game, you were cut out completely. Silent treatment, cold shoulder, and potentially a future target. Athena joked, "You'll be sent to Outcast Island."

Nobody wanted that. A fate worse than death, we used to think . . . until we saw actual death, or at least its aftermath. Not the scream, but the echo of it. What do scientists call it? The aftershock? Once you felt that shiver down in your bones, the cold permanency of oblivion, a few days on Outcast Island didn't seem half so bad.

We treated it as a joke.

I can't deny it. I know this makes me sound like the biggest jerk on the globe, but it was funny at first. We laughed about it. We tried to write the nastiest, filthiest, wildest comments possible. It was a challenge, and we all looked forward to reading the next crazy message. A lot of people were reading it at first. We loved when something got a big reaction in school.

For example:

I'd rather crawl inside an aardvark's asshole than spend two minutes with you.

That's creative and humorous, at least I thought so at the time. Other people wrote way meaner. I had a hard time deciding which animal it should be: a rhinoceros, grasshopper, donkey, chicken, and so on. (Decisions, decisions.) At first I used the word *poophole*, but I changed it at the last minute. Who can know for sure. Art is so subjective.

After a while, most of us just got bored.

I am, you should realize by now, a complete idiot.

SUPER AWKWARD

Our teachers said that it sometimes helped to talk about these things. Share feelings, exchange ideas. Whatever happens, don't keep it buried inside or you might blow like a volcano. *Ga-zoom.*

(Wait, is that the sound volcanoes make? *Ga-zoom?* Seriously doubtful. I suck at onomatopoeia. Carry on!)

It seemed like three out of every five teachers felt a need to say something wise and important. They gazed at us through sincere eye sockets. We got all quiet and tried to make it look like we were searching our souls instead of secretly watching the clock.

Grief counselors visited the school those first few days and "made themselves available." It was super awkward. One morning announcement said there would be an open gathering after school, where students could go to talk, hang out, share memories, and "enjoy" refreshments.

For reasons I can't explain, I thought this might be a good idea. Or, I guess, the right thing to do. That's the problem. Nobody knew the right thing to do. We didn't have any experience.

The gathering was in the old lower gym—and the minute I walked in I knew it was a mistake. There were way too many teachers holding clear plastic cups, milling around in hushed tones.

There weren't many students there, and I was one of the few guys. I estimated twenty tops. Morgan Mallen wasn't super popular.

One huddle of girls stood around sobbing and patting each other on the shoulder. I took a deep breath and headed for the refreshment table.

Soon an unknown, walrus-like teacher appeared beside me as I scarfed my second fudge brownie.

"You're Sam, right?"

"Yeah, yes," I said.

He was a lumpy man in a way-too-cheerful sweater. And I mean *waaaaay*. It was like a peacock exploded on it. Neon barf. He wore a thick, droopy mustache. Beads of sweat glistened on his forehead. Like some weird alien, the sweaty walrus beamed a chipped-tooth smile directly into my eyeballs. I got zapped by Mr. Sensitivity.

"I'm Mr. Laneway, one of the social workers here at school." He extended a hand. This was awkward, because my hands were full with apple juice (right hand) and brownie (left hand), and he was all, "Oh, oh, your hands are full, never mind, it's fine," before I figured that I could free up my left hand by balancing the brownie in the crook of my right elbow. I gave him my hand, upside down and backward.

(Genius.)

After the handshake ritual was complete, I made for the exit.

"You won the essay contest last year," Mr. Laneway said. "I remember."

This took me off guard. How did he know?

"I was one of the judges," he explained. "Your composition really stood out. Excellent work. It felt honest."

"Thanks, thank you," I said and really hoped we had reached the end of our conversation. Last stop! Everyone off the bus!

"I hope you're still writing," Mr. Laneway said. "You have talent, Sam."

I shifted on my feet. I didn't ordinarily love this kind of under-the-spotlight deal. He wasn't a creep or anything—I mean, he was actually saying nice things—but I wanted to be invisible about the whole writing thing. Keep it on the down low. I never should have entered that contest.

"You probably want to join the others," Mr. Laneway observed.

(Yes, I super do!)

"You should try keeping a journal," he suggested. "It's important, at times like this, to have a place to go with your thoughts and feelings."

I gave him a blank look.

He waited, wanting more.

"Maybe I'll try it," I said.

"Please know, Sam, that you are welcome to come by my office anytime if you"—his perfectly round head tilted east, then west, then east again—"if you want to discuss things or, you know, talk about Morgan, or—"

"Yeah, I mean, yes! That'd be great, thanks," I sputtered. "I might."

(Unlikely!)

Mrs. Kalman, the principal, asked for us to all gather around. (Except she said, "Gather *round*," though I don't completely get why.)

She made some important and serious remarks in an official manner. Clearly Mrs. Kalman was trying to say all the right things, but it felt artificial to me, like the orange soda at Walmart. I totally regretted coming to this meeting /gathering/get-together thingy. All the adults were just way too eager to be sensitive and supportive. I kept wanting to shout, "Minimize, minimize!"

I faded in with a small group of students, quasi-friends and familiar faces. Mrs. Kalman talked and we listened, still numb. I don't think anybody knew how to act, even the adults—or maybe *especially* the adults. The bizarre thing is that I felt perfectly normal in so many ways. I woke up, ate the standard amount of frozen waffles (four, starving!), rode the bus (groan), laughed when something funny happened in school—then immediately felt bad about laughing, because it was so obviously wrong to be alive and happy at a time like this. There was a weird vacuum suck inside me, like an air bubble under water, and I felt like, I don't know, I had to burp all the time. But I couldn't. I just walked around with that swollen, full-up, burpy feeling. The pressure building, building.

A school counselor spoke. She gestured to a table with stacks of papers and fancy pamphlets and told us that we should consider taking this time to fill out one of the worksheets. She said it might be a good mental exercise. I grabbed one, to be exactly like everybody else, thinking: *Burpies for brains, this is so yuck.* I folded the sheet and stuffed it into my pocket. Some girls actually took out pencils and chewed on their erasers in a thoughtful manner. I grabbed another brownie—sue me: they were *really* good!—and waited for this grim gathering to conclude. When they asked us to hand in our activity sheets at the end, I was all, "Huh, what?"

I guess I didn't really see the point. They treated us like we needed to be cured or fixed or something. I don't know, maybe they were right about it. But this didn't feel like the way to get it done. It did get me thinking about Morgan, though. And if it makes anybody out there happy, I had a hard time getting to sleep that night.

THE FIRST TIME

This is how we met. It happened by accident, late in October, months after she had become Athena Luikin's favorite target.

So I'm saying: This is the first time I talked to the real person. Not just through the internet or as the nearly invisible person drifting through the school halls. I mean the real girl.

I looked Morgan in the eyes, made her laugh, saw her smile, heard her voice, smelled her shampoo. I'm trying to say that she became real to me. That should have changed things. I know that. I know how it makes me look. And I really know how it makes me *feel*. But let's forget about that for now. Let's focus on . . . not me.

It was the Pumpkin Fest, and I had volunteered to help out. Well, okay, not true. My mother signed me up and told me I was doing it.

"No choice?" I protested.

"No choice," she answered.

"That's not fair," I said.

"I pay your monthly phone bill," she countered.

So I volunteered to help out at the Pumpkin Fest. I figured it couldn't be too terrible. I like little kids as long as they 1) don't try to bite me; 2) don't have goobers running down their noses; and 3) don't act like little brainiacs who want to tell me all about dinosaurs or *Star Wars* or whatever (though, yes, I can talk the history of Marvel Comics all day long).

I've got a little brother and sister at home and I'll say it: I love those guys almost all the time. Which is a pretty high percentage, if you think about it. I've compared notes with other brothers, so I know what I'm talking about.

At the Pumpkin Fest, I hoped I'd get assigned to the corn maze or the haunted house, something cool like that, where I could jump out with a plastic chain saw in my hand and scare the candy corn out of those kids. That, I would enjoy. *Bwa-ha-ha-ha!* Giving four-year-olds a cardiac arrest? I'm all in.

So it sucked when I was told to go over to the Face Painting Station.

"Seriously?" I asked.

I received an enthusiastic nod from a seriously coffeed-up yoga mom. She was like the queen of volunteers and actually had a clipboard tucked into her armpit.

"I'm no Picasso," I said.

"It's easy," she assured me. Big smile, blazing white teeth, crazy stiff hair, bony arms. "The kids want stars or pumpkins or rainbows. Simple stuff. There's a sheet you can follow."

I hesitated.

"You'll have fun," she lied, and shoved me in the direction of the Face Painting Station.

It's hard to say no to an enthusiastic yoga mom. After all, I had volunteered, which was like showing up with a giant "YES!" markered across my forehead.

I trekked over to the picnic table, which was surrounded by a ragged bunch of twerps. I wondered if the PTA ladies realized that they basically created a training class for the future tattooed freaks of America.

Morgan was painting a jack-o'-lantern on the pudgy face of a freckled, red-haired girl. It was pretty sweet, actually, the way that little girl stood with her arms frozen to her sides, trying to hold herself so perfectly still.

"Does your nose itch?" I asked the little girl.

Her eyes narrowed as a new worry entered her skull.

I made a big show of scratching my nose very dramatically. "It's hard to hold still when your nose itches, don't you think?"

The little girl's rabbity nose twitched. Her shoulders wriggled.

"Don't listen to him," Morgan said, grinning. "You can scratch if you want."

The station consisted of a picnic table and a hand-lett

sign that read, you guessed it: FACE PAINTING STATION. An assortment of paints was scattered on the table, a total mess, very haphazard, if you ask me. An untidy line of future gang members stood anxiously waiting their turn with the fake tattoos.

"So, um," I pointed back in the direction of the hyper mom, "she said I should come over to help out."

Morgan put the finishing touches on the redhead's chubby cheek. "There you go," she said, holding up a hand mirror. "What do you think? Do you like it?"

The kid nodded solemnly. She asked, "Will it come off?"

Not missing a beat, Morgan replied, "Yes, it will wear off in a year or two."

The kid's eyes bulged out like a cartoon character after it realizes that it's raced off a cliff. Nothing but air under its feet. Scooby-Doo's "Ruh-roh." Funny.

Morgan smiled. "I'm joking. A little soap and water will wash it off."

The relieved kid waddled over toward the cupcakes.

"Can you paint a spider on this girl's face?" Morgan asked me.

And that was the first time we ever talked.

It was about a spider on the day I sat down beside her.

Clever, huh?

SOMEBODY ELSE

I sometimes daydream about becoming somebody else. Anybody else.

Not me.

I imagine how I might lose myself, my old self. Shed it like a winter coat on the first warm spring day. I'd become something new. Something free.

I'd be older, with a car, and I'd drive around from state to state, a nameless drifter hitting all the nowhere towns. I'd get a series of mindless jobs that didn't matter. Maybe I'd work as a dishwasher somewhere, happy to punch the clock, or I'd find construction work with a roofer, like my cousin Tim. I'd haul heavy packages of shingles on my shoulder and climb high ladders. Develop serious muscles, get all ripped and studly. I'd wear floppy hats, bang nails till sun-down, shirtless and tan, not a thought in my head. Just haul-ing and banging, stopping for lunch and sunscreen, then hauling and banging some more. I wouldn't have to think. I'd meet people who didn't know anything about the old me—I would be a clean slate. There would be no "I." And I, this person with the pen, would become whatever anyone wanted me to be.

"Do you like electronic music?" somebody might ask.

And I'd smile real big. "Oh, yeah! You bet I do!"

Even when the old me might have thought, *Hell no I don't!*

I'd be happy. For a while, at least. Then I'd feel that old yank of the heart, you know, gotta move on. The mysterious drifter. I'd shove off to some other place, maybe steal a little money along the way, not too much, nothing crazy, break into a house while rich folks slept, grab enough to get by till I found a new job somewhere. And I'd invent myself a new life, in a new place, and maybe even fall in love. Or better still, find someone, anyone, who could fall in love with me.

She'd ask my name.

And I'd look into her pretty blue eyes and say, "Baby doll, I don't even know who in the world I am."

THE SHRINE

At the shrine, there's lots of things.
Teddy bears, flowers, candles, rings.

Somebody left a CD case, maybe a song
in there meant something, I don't know.

Pink strings, heart-shaped balloons, hand-made
friendship bracelets, photographs, white

Crosses, ballet slippers, notes about now
being in a far better place, the letters

"R.I.P." constructed with duct tape and
aluminum foil, a T-shirt signed by every girl

That's ever walked the earth, and on and on
it went, everybody leaving their mark,

Their scent, I was here, I peed on this tree,
see how much, how deeply, how dearly I care.

I just stand and stare and stare. No tears
come, but my teeth clench. I remember

thinking: *I don't know if I can do this.*

WHAT'S DONE IS DONE

I had a talk with Fergus today. Morgan had been gone for a week. Dead and buried. Most of the shock had worn off, and things shifted back to normal. Newspaper reports talked about how she was "terrorized on social media," but nothing more had come of it.

No "bullies" were named.

Rumors flew, but the cops didn't arrest anybody. Morgan's parents didn't seem interested in pressing charges. They kept to themselves.

We were all relieved.

The news moved on to the next disaster. A typhoon in the Philippines . . . Killer wasps in China . . . A shooting in a mall somewhere in Texas . . . Another celebrity in rehab.

The coast was clearing.

I was worried anyway. Before I climbed on the bus after school, I saw Fergus by the bike racks. "Do you think the police will find out about . . . you know?"

Fergus didn't even turn his head to look at me. He kept spinning the numbers of his combination lock.

I persisted. "I mean, obviously they know. But will they find out who posted those things? Can they trace a computer's IP address or whatever?"

"Those sites are encrypted. It's anonymous. That's the whole point, Sherlock. Besides," he added, wrapping the chain around his seat, snapping the lock shut, "I don't know what you're talking about, Sam. What did you do?"

(What did *I* do?)

It hit me like a baseball bat. Right on the sweet spot.

Fergus spat. "I wasn't involved in any of that shit."

"But—"

He stood tall, the bike frame resting against his muscled thigh. Fergus placed a powerful grip on my shoulder. He glared, leaned close, and spoke softly, hardly above a whisper. "Listen, Sam, friend. I don't know what you're talking about. And I don't care. What's done is done. So shut up. Okay? I mean it. Don't ever, ever, ever talk about this again. Not to me, not to anyone."

Fergus pulled back his right hand and gave me a short punch to my chest. Not a hard one, but a message just the same. Two words: Shut up. And two more: Or else.

A voice called and Fergus waved to someone behind me. I glanced over my shoulder to see Athena Luikin waiting by the main doors. She stood looking at us, arms crossed below her perfect breasts, long blond hair, mouth tight. I raised my hand, howdy, but she offered no reply. Queen bees don't often greet the drones.

My brain roared like the sound of ocean waves against a rocky shore, a blur of white noise. I was enveloped in fog. Suddenly the sky cleared, the sun came out. I could see how it was going to go.

The plan was set.

We were going to deny everything . . . and it was all going to be okay.

BLANK

Today
I got nothing.

FILLING IN THE BLANKS

Remember the activity sheet I took from school? The mental gymnastics that were supposed to help me heal? I guess I shoved that sheet in my desk drawer. I'm staring at the crumpled thing right now, here in my bedroom.

1) The person who died in my life is . . .

a) Um, dead?
b) Morgan Mallen.
c) A girl I kind of knew?

2) The cause of death was . . .

a) The ground.
b) How much time have you got?
c) I don't know why she did it. I mean, depression, I guess, but I can't imagine.

3) I found out about the death when . . .

I got a text.

4) After death, I believe my loved one is . . .

a) Wait, "loved one"?
b) Is this really a question about the afterlife? I guess I don't really see her on a fluffy cloud surrounded by harpists with wings.
c) Relieved it's over.

5) My first feeling was . . . because . . .

a) Is "shock" a feeling? It felt like a non-feeling to me, no feeling at all. Because: I felt dead too?
b) You know, there's something else, now that I think about it. I was excited. I mean, it was big news, this huge thing that happened, so I started texting like crazy and Twitter exploded. As gross as this sounds, there was

an initial thrill to it. I can't tell you how that depresses me to this day.

6) Now I feel . . . because . . .

a) Like crap because: duh.
b) Angry because: THIS FORM!

7) What makes me feel most angry?

a) How did you know?
b) The phonies all around me.
c) That she did this to herself, that it got to this point, that . . . next.

8) I worry about . . . because . . .

a) What happens next, "because" duh.
b) Me, "because" everything completely sucks, like who cares.

9) The hardest thing about school is . . . because . . .

a) Is this is a trick question? Next!
b) The fake feeling everywhere, the way her locker is now a shrine.
c) The walk from science to band, where I used to always see her.
d) All the things I never said.

10) My friends are . . .

a) Clueless.
b) Guilty too.
c) Kind of scary.

11) The adults in my life tell me . . .

a) I'm sorry, I wasn't listening. What?
b) That filling out forms is a good "mental exercise."
c) It's best to "move on."

12) What helps me most is . . .

a) This stupid form. Kidding!
b) Television=very helpful.
c) I wish I knew the answer to this one. Truly.
d) Wait! My journal? Those blank pages? Writing?

13) What helps me the least is . . .

a) Pretending I didn't care.
b) All those plastic people pretending they do.

PEOPLE TALKING

I heard the talkers talking,
expressing all they knew
& didn't know

—she was stupid,
she was sick,
she was selfish, brave,
twisted, stoned, splattered;
she left a note,
she didn't leave a note;
how she jumped off
the water tower at the edge
of the woods, and how
Demarcus joked, "Damn,
she killed that hang-
out spot, but seriously!"

I tried not to speak,
and surely didn't laugh,
just nodded and drifted, drifted, drifted
away like the flicked ash
from somebody's cigarette.

STILL NOTHING

The color scheme of our school revolves around three basic colors: puke green, urine stain, and variations of beige. Each year, we spent exactly one hundred and eighty days inside that wonderful building. Snow days didn't count, but half days did, even when Mr. Cranston only showed YouTube videos in social studies (true story!). We waited for time to spill, like liquid from a stabbed water balloon or blood from a cut sleeve.

Then we were set free.

In one of our last texts, Morgan wrote that she hated every one of those one hundred and eighty days. She couldn't face the idea of the same dumb day on repeat.

So I guess that's partly why she ended up doing what she did. At least the timing of it.

But still.

There had to be more, right?

And *every single day*? That was harsh. There was not even *one good day* out of one hundred eighty? It was hard to believe, mathematically speaking, considering the odds of it. Every day? Really, Morgan?

She wasn't thinking straight.

(Obviously.)

I didn't want to believe her.

(And it hurt a little too.)

I happen to know otherwise. There were good days, good times. Moments when, you know, she was happy.

(Or seemed to be, or faked it good.)

When I think about what it took for her to step off that water tower, the physical act of stepping out and stepping into emptiness, into the airy sky?

When I think of that, really picture it in my mind, then yeah, she must have meant it. To her, it was truth.

The moment before she fell, at least, she believed.

I'll say this:

Morgan had guts.

I still wonder though. What did she think when she was falling midair, legs kicking, arms pinwheeling? Rag-dolling through the universe? Was there a scream of remorse? Or did she go down like a sack, a silent fall followed by a muffled thud?

These are the things I think about when I'm alone and I turn out the lights. Lately I've been falling asleep with my headphones on, the music paving over my thoughts.

ACCIDENT

I didn't do it,
not me . . .

She was sick,
anybody could see . . .

To take things so
seriously.

THE TOWER GETS TAGGED

A new rumor ran wild through school today. Morgan's shrine had been vandalized over the weekend. Objects that had been left—balloons, photographs, lousy stuffed teddy bears—were destroyed, sympathy cards scattered everywhere. I heard it was a real mess. Somebody spray-painted on the side of the water tower, "BITCH DESERVED IT!"

No one could believe it. I mean, what the hell? More tears, more crying. Everyone acted shocked and horrified and outraged. And I guess we were, some of us.

I'm pretty sure I know who did it.

Athena doesn't even pretend to be upset. "We weren't friends, everybody knows that," I heard her say.

Hate is an amazing thing. Some days it feels like hate makes the world go round. Other days, hate takes a day off—and stupidity steps in.

My stomach is empty; my brain's spitting exhaust. I feel like I'm on a boat in choppy waters, watching my guts heave over the railing. Food for the sharks.

ALONE, TOGETHER

The second time I was alone with Morgan it was a couple of weeks past Pumpkin Fest. We were in the open grounds in the far back behind school, which happened to occupy a midpoint between both our houses. I had taken my chocolate lab, Max, and was blasting tennis balls into the stratosphere. Almost eight years old, Max still loved nothing better than chasing after those fuzzy green balls and bringing them back to me. Labs are hardwired that way: retrieve and please, retrieve and please. I wouldn't call Max an intellectual.

I actually enjoyed it, hitting those balls as far as I could and watching Max run and run. With Max and me, there was never any drama. No BS. *Whack,* I sent another ball flying, and Max bounded after it. The ball soared far and bounced high. Max leaped and snagged it on the first hop. I wish I had a mad vertical like that.

Even an athlete like Max gets tired after a while. I checked my phone while Max sniffed and selected a few trees to water.

Bark-bark-bark-bark, bark! Bark-bark, barky-BARKY bark-bark!

A miniature white mop-like *thing* charged at me like a high-pitched, furry lunatic.

"Sorry, sorry, sorry!" a voice called out.

I looked and it was her, walking in my direction. Morgan collared the dog, still apologizing. "Sorry, Larry barks at everybody. I keep hoping he'll get over it, but . . ." There was no point finishing the sentence. She let it die there in the grass.

"Larry?" I asked.

"Yeah, why?" There was toughness in her voice. Defenses dialed all the way up.

"Nothing," I said. "I like it."

Her expression softened.

Max came over to check out the yappy dog. "Max, meet Larry," I said, getting the introductions out of the way.

Morgan scratched Max around the neck and head. Max leaned against her legs gratefully, surrendering to the affection. The little mop-freak dog kept jealously *barkBARKbarking*.

I stared at my phone, scrolled.

Morgan pulled her cell out of a coat pocket.

We stood there in awkward proximity, alone on a field, playing games with our phones. Silence drifted over us like clouds.

I pocketed the cell.

"Bye," I said.

I don't remember if she answered me, but Morgan called to Max, "See ya, boy!"

DANCE LESSONS

I found out she took dance lessons after school. Tuesdays and Thursdays. She loved her dog. But mostly, her parents told the reporters, she liked quiet things. Staying home, playing board games—board games! I didn't know that—which ones, I wonder?—and watching movies.

So maybe not so different after all.

Now that she's gone, I think about those dance lessons. She must have gone to one of those places in town, "Miss Genevieve's" or "The Jazz Experience." It could be where she first encountered Athena. Hmm. Was that the beginning of the end? I never got the full details. Some fight over a boy. I imagine Morgan all happy and excited in her spandex tutu or whatever she wore, muffin top poking out in lumps. She wasn't a super-pretty girl. A little thick, especially toward the summer, when she gained a lot of weight. Like she stopped caring altogether. But when I picture her now in my memory, moving silently through the halls, arms crossed over her books, head down, not meeting anyone's eyes, I think maybe she did have a certain dancer's grace beneath it all. There were days I found myself following her down the hall. We had the same math class, and both of us had the same long walk to band at the other end of the building.

I'd sometimes settle in behind her—not directly, but more the way a sly detective tails a guy in a car—holding back a few spots, changing lanes, keeping things under my hat. Her shoulders were sloped, roundish, as if she hoped to pull herself into a ball. There were times, though, when maybe she forgot herself—or forgot everybody else, I guess—and she walked tall, head high, and I could see that she was actually beautiful, no matter what anybody said.

For, you know, a social outcast everyone hated.

We never once spoke in school.

Not once.

I SEE HER FLYING WITHOUT WINGS

That's when I finally stammer
hello

& she's gone.

THE GODDESS

I can't explain Athena's power without stating the obvious.

She was beautiful. I mean, *smoking*. Everybody knew it. You couldn't *not* look at Athena Luikin. The blond hair, the lips, her flawless skin, and tight body. Athena was a legend from the time when five different elementary schools came together in one building.

The guys talked.

"Have you seen . . . ?"

"She's in my English class."

"Smoking hot."

She was the original sexy girl in our lives. Athena's outward appearance gave her celebrity and power. It's easy to see now that Athena had issues of her own. Inside that spectacular body there was, I suppose, an ordinary person with the usual assortment of flaws and insecurities. Back in the early days of middle school, she seemed like a gift from Mount Olympus, so the guys were all willing to accept a certain level of elitist behavior. We just naturally assumed she was better than us and, really, on many levels, she just was. To this day, I'm not sure why girls follow her lead, but they do. Maybe everybody gives "pretty" too much credit.

Athena hated (hated, *hated*!) Morgan Mallen and made it her life's mission to make Morgan as miserable as possible. And when it came to dealing out misery, Athena had a natural gift for it. I'm saying she was *good* at it.

Look, that's life. There are always going to be unpopular people in the world—and everybody knows that girls can be so cruel. Sure, guys can be brutal too. There's some big dummies walking around, knuckles dragging. I once watched Dominick Demeri beat Eddie Santana to a bloody pulp just for cutting his legs out from under him on the basketball court. It wasn't intentional, but Dominick didn't see it that way. He went a little crazy. The next day, life moved on, and after Eddie got out of the hospital, nobody thought about it much. I didn't anyway.

Athena had a different style. With one withering remark, she could shred someone's soul into thin strips. She'd tease the jugular vein out of your throat, sprinkle sugar on it, and suck it down like a raw oyster while you watched.

Athena was relentless. Each night, she'd dream up new ways of torturing her enemies—new lies, new hurts, new games. She never stopped, like in *Terminator 3: Rise of the Machines* (the crappy one with the chill blonde who plays the T-X that's been sent back to kill John Connor's . . . oh, never mind).

Long after lesser people might have moved on to the next thing, Athena kept putting on the pressure until some sick, mean instinct inside her felt satisfied.

For at least an entire year, probably more, Morgan was target #1 on Athena's hate list. I'm not really sure why. I heard rumors. Morgan talked to the wrong guy. Maybe something happened between them, or not. Morgan and Athena might have been friends once. I don't know exactly, not sure I even want to know. Some crazy female drama. The main thing is this: Athena tagged a bull's-eye on Morgan's back, labeled her a slut, then handed out weapons to the rest of us.

You know what we basically said?

(This is the killer.)

"Sure, if we can be your friend!"

We all wanted to be friends with Athena Luikin. After all, she was a goddess in tight jeans and a North Face jacket.

COULD HAVE SAID

Some things I could have said but didn't:

> *"You are not alone."*
> *"Things will get better."*
> *"I care about you."*
> *"Your life is important."*
> *"I am here for you."*

Things I said:

> *"You are a fat ugly beast."*

Those are the facts, folks.

THE LIBRARY

The first time we laughed together was a Saturday or Sunday in November. I had gone to the town library with my mom. She went to look at the "Hot New Fiction" shelves, and I wandered over to the videos. I remember I was in the W section—scanning *World War Z*, *War of the Worlds*, whatever—and Morgan kind of quietly came up and said, "I saw that thing you did."

And I was like, "What the what?" I didn't expect to see her there, in public, and I didn't realize we were on speaking terms.

"At the sliding doors," she said. There was something playful in her voice, like she was enjoying this. "That thing you did with your hand."

Oh, that. When I walk up to an automatic door, like at the supermarket or the library, I try to perfectly time a wave of my hand to make it feel like I'm magically opening the door.

I know, it's stupid. I'm an idiot. That's been established.

"I didn't think anyone was watching," I confessed.

"So what's that about?" she asked, grinning.

My cheeks felt warm, like blood was rushing into them. "It's Obi-Wan Kenobi," I reluctantly explained. "You know, '*These aren't the droids you're looking for.*' "

She gave me a blank stare. "Is that a movie quote?"

She had no clue what I was talking about.

"*Star Wars, Episode Four,* which is really the first one," I said. I gestured with my hand and said in my best Obi-Wan voice, "*You don't need to see his identification.*"

Nothing, no reaction.

"You've seen *Star Wars*, haven't you?"

She shrugged. "Yeah, maybe. I know what it is, it's not like I live under a rock. I just don't think I've ever watch-watched it."

"Watch-watched it?" I laughed. "As opposed to . . . ?"

"When the TV's on but you're not really watching," she said, "and you eventually change the channel."

"Seriously?"

"In case you haven't noticed, I'm not a nerdy dad in dork jeans," she said. "I'm a normal teenage girl—we don't care about *Star Wars.*"

(*Normal?* Yeah, I heard that too.)

"I'm not a dad either," I pointed out, "but I loved those movies when I was a kid."

She lifted up on her toes and chirped, "I bet ten bucks your father made you watch them, like it was some important bonding ritual. A guy thing."

"He did!" I laughed. "It was a really big deal for us. I can remember it like it was yesterday—he even let me drink orange soda!"

"It's called brainwashing," she said. "You owe me ten bucks."

"I didn't bet."

"Pay up," she said, palm out.

At that point, more people crowded in the aisle between the shelves. I saw my mother heading in our direction and felt weirdly exposed. So I quickly grabbed a movie, any movie, and mumbled, "Gotta go."

She already had a horror movie in her hand, studying the back of it. "Seen it?" she asked.

"Yeah, no." I shrugged.

A small wave of my hand, Obi-Wan-like, and *poof,* I was gone.

We never got the hang of good-byes.

ABOUT ME

I remember reading that Max was the most popular name for dogs in America. The second most popular was Daisy.

You already know the name of my dog.

The incredibly lame thing is that I was originally going to call him Daisy, until my parents explained that she was actually a he and might feel uncomfortable with a girl's name. My dad said, "Like the Johnny Cash song, 'A Boy Named Sue.'"

(Whatever, Dad, with your endless geezer references.)

So I thought and thought until I came up with Max. Because I'm a genius, right? A true original, that's me.

If you are looking for unique and amazing—a trailblazer, an adventurer—then you better get moving. Because I'm not that guy. I'm pretty average. Maybe a little below average, honestly. Except for my height. I'm tall for my age, almost six feet and growing like a weed, as my mom likes to say.

I've never had a girlfriend. Basically, girls terrify me, especially the good-looking ones. My brain goes slack. My tongue swells to the size of a kitchen sponge. Any words I summon come out like, "Bluh, urg, blork, splurge." Other times when I get near a girl, I power down completely. No Wi-Fi, no signal. I got nothing. That's just the way I am. I stare at the floor and blink and blink and blink.

But with Morgan, it was different, maybe because I didn't see her that way. Not at first, maybe not ever. It's confusing to explain and, by now, pretty pointless.

I'm a follower, if you want to know the truth. What can I say? I'm happy when I can hang out with the guys, fall in with a crowd, sit down at a lunch table that has jokes and laughter and a few upscale kids. I don't want to be in charge of anything. Which is good, because I'm *so not,* and I'm happy that way. Leave the decisions to somebody else. I'm happy going along for the ride.

Used to be, anyway.

I LOOKED AWAY

I've replayed this next scene over in my mind a hundred times, a thousand times. It was the week after I ran into Morgan at the town library. I was walking down the busy, crowded hallway between periods with some friends. I looked up and there she was, books pressed against her body like a shield, arms crisscrossed like a fullback carrying the ball toward the goal line. She was alone and her head was down, shoulders hunched in that way she had. Maybe she sensed me, I don't know. But Morgan looked up as we passed. Her eyes flickered.

I saw her see me.

Her lips parted almost imperceptibly . . . and there was something . . . something in her eyes.

"Cow," Tim Early uttered.

"Moo, moo, moooooooooo," Jeff Castellano lowed, followed by snickers and various barn noises. Chickens clucking, roosters crowing, the snorting of pigs. The laughter came like razors.

Morgan's cheeks flushed crimson. Her head down, she pushed forward and plunged through. Down the long hallway, down and away. The laughter had sliced her up, cut her to ribbons.

But not before her eyes met mine. For one sliver of a moment, one split second, she looked at me in horror and wonderment, amid the cruelty and the laughter. Maybe she wondered what I'd do. If I'd nod or smile or say a word.

If I'd even recognize that she existed, this person I had laughed with just a few days before.

All I did that day was look away.

It's all I ever did.

I looked away.

I was not the droid she was looking for.

NOT ME

Ladies and gentlemen of the jury, please allow me to introduce myself. I am not a bully.

I almost wrote "a man of wealth and taste," hearing that Rolling Stones tune in my head, Dad's classic rock CDs.

But that's a song about being the devil, it couldn't possibly apply here.

Um.

Samuel Proctor is not the guy you might imagine. Sure, you might prefer to stuff me into a box, pin a tail on me, label and define me. But I'm not that guy—*the bully*, the evil one, destroyer of souls, enemy of the state, may he rot in hell.

I'm more than that.

For starters, and I know this sounds exceedingly lame, but I love my mom. Love her. I'm a big brother. I take care of my dog, I'm a good friend, a great teammate (even if I'm not an awesome player). When you go up to the plate, I'm rooting for you. When you strike out, I'm the guy who says, "You'll get 'em next time," or "Damn, that was a nasty curveball—unhittable."

Even if I'm not in the game, I'm the first one to warm up the right fielder between innings.

Ask anybody.

I'm a nice guy.

You can't take one thing I did—a dumb thing, for sure—and then use that to define me forever.

I made a mistake.

I screwed up. (Let's see you be perfect 24/7.)

Okay, yes, I confess: It wasn't technically "one time." It was more accurately a series of mistakes.

I let things go too far. I should have done more to stop it. I could have . . .

(Should have, could have.)

If you do one screwed-up thing, does that become the sum total of your life? Of course not, that's crazy. Across a lifetime, we do billions of things. Zillions of things, as many things as there are stars in the universe.

I guess it depends on the one thing, right? I sent a few cruel messages. I could have been kinder okay, granted. It doesn't make me a bully forever. Someday I want to go to college, get married, be a father, have kids, maybe become a lawyer or even a writer. Save lives, work for the environment, travel the world, have adventures. Maybe even, you know, *do good.*

She jumped.

She did it, don't forget that while you sit in judgment. And, absolutely, I *hate* Morgan for doing that. What was she thinking? She obviously had problems, and I got caught up in her messy life. I feel terrible about it. Not even about my role (forget me!), but for her. It slays me that she did that to herself.

Bad thought: I wonder if murderers feel the same way as I do? You know, like, "I stabbed a homeless person eight times in the neck—but other than that, I'm a really sweet guy!"

Ha.

Or *ugh.*

Can an otherwise all-around great bunch of guys, for example, take advantage of a drunk girl at a party? No way. You do something like that, you suck forever. Your soul goes up in flames. But we hear about it on the news, don't we? Some poor girl gets into a situation with some Neanderthal guys and there's nobody around with the courage to lift a finger in her defense. Bunch of bystanders. "Huh? Who? What?"

We hear about a kid who takes a hatchet to both of his parents. When the police finally cart him away, splattered in blood, there's always (*always*!) a clueless neighbor interviewed on the evening news who shakes his head and says, "He was such a nice boy. Quiet and polite. Never met a sweeter child in my life."

I guess you can fool most of the people most of the time.

But can you fool yourself?

Can you fool the universe?

So I'm saying, yeah, I get it: If you kill somebody, I don't care what else you've done with your life, you're basically a crappy person. The one act defines you forever.

Murderer.

So is that it with me?

Did she jump?

Or was she pushed?

I guess the question is this:

Did I help push her? Was that my hand against her back?

What if I'm just another rubber dummy who watched?

(Huh? Who? What?)

Who am I? What am I?

I still don't know.

"GO," SHE SAID

When we met, we were usually out walking our dogs. Never on purpose, exactly. I normally took Max for a quick trip around the block. But some days, maybe hoping to see her, I'd head back over to the middle school where I could let Max off-leash. Dogs have a way of letting you know what they like, and Max loved that free-to-roam feeling.

It was best in the frozen winter, when only hardcore dog lovers stood around hoping their toes wouldn't snap off. Sometimes I'd see Morgan a long way off, leaving in the other direction while I was coming down the hill where I cut through the woods, and I'd watch her leave. Other days our timing would be great. Always by accident, never planned. We hadn't yet crossed that line. Funny thing, our dogs became friends before we did. We kind of stood there, watching the dogs sniff each other's butts, and I'd think that it was pretty cool I wasn't a dog. A simple nod or handshake was more than enough for me.

The dogs helped us along, I think, gave us things to talk about. We were becoming *something,* though it was hard to say what.

(Friends?)

I liked being around her, which was weird, because she was the first girl I ever spoke easily with on my own, who wasn't like a cousin or some girl down the block. Morgan was still unusual, I guess, but I was getting used to her mood swings. She'd get quiet sometimes. What's the word? *Sullen.* Morgan had an *inside* quality, like she lived in her head a lot. (I don't know. Does that make sense?) But overall, she seemed regular to me. And, at other times, pretty lively.

There was one time we were together, out on the empty field. It was early December, the days getting shorter. The branches of the trees were bare, the grass brown and sad. The promise of snow was in the cold, moist air. That's how it is with snow, you can feel it before it comes. Maybe other things are like that too, I don't know. Looking out, I spied a group of guys coming around the corner. I knew them and felt instantly uneasy, standing in the middle of nowhere, talking to Public Enemy #1.

I interrupted Morgan. "Yeah, look. I better get—"

Her eyes went from me to the guys and back to me again. And in that second, I saw the resignation in her face and watched her features collapse.

"Go," she said, her voice flat.

"What?"

"Go!"

Her voice was raw now. I could hear the hurt.

I paused.

She said, "I don't want to *embarrass* you, Sam."

I whistled for old Max and moved out fast, hoping no one saw us, on earth or in heaven.

Those are the things I regret the most, now that she's gone. The little things I did and didn't do.

(Someday I have to stop being a coward.)

I WAS IT

My heart dive-bombed into my stomach, *thwapp-splurch,* when I found the note in my locker. Seriously, it felt like a loon had been shot out of the sky. *Ka-boom,* and feathers flew. Open season.

TAG, YOUR TURN.

I held the blue poster board, glanced around to see that nobody was watching, and stuffed it back underneath my science textbook.

I had forgotten about the game. Or at least managed to push it out of my mind. It had been more than a month since I'd been involved. Now it was my turn again to post the next message. The clock was ticking.

This time it felt different, now that I kind of knew her.

What should I do?

I considered my options. I could ignore it, pretend I never received the instructions. Do nothing, play dumb. I knew instantly it would never work. Athena had selected me. Athena would be watching.

I didn't want to do anything that might attract attention. No one knew that I was now friendly with Morgan Mallen. It was a secret—something outside of the everyday world of school—and I wanted to keep it that way. I knew that once other people got involved, it would ruin everything between us. If I stood up for Morgan now, they might come after me. And what good would that do?

I tried talking to Jeff Castellano after school. Test the general vibe. Jeff and I played on a couple of travel baseball teams together the past few years and were friends, in a never-really-hanging-out-much kind of way. He was a catcher, mostly because Jeff genuinely liked squatting in the dirt. It gave him the best view of the game. Jeff *looked* like a catcher too. In other words: stocky, pudgy, stout. But strong. That's something I learned in life: You can't beat the short, round guys in a fight, because they are made of rubber. Nothing hurts them. So as a rule I tried not to piss off Jeff Castellano.

I was the opposite—a string bean in sneakers, an undernourished flagpole. When Jeff and I stood side by side, people said it was like looking at the number ten. Which was pretty funny, if you think about it.

I didn't tell Jeff about Morgan exactly. I just kind of expressed doubts about all the mean things we'd been doing online.

"You promise you won't tell anyone?" I asked.

Jeff shrugged. "Sure, whatever. But you've got it all wrong. She *likes* it."

"I don't know . . ."

"No one made her open that account," Jeff said. He sipped on an "extra-thick" milkshake with the urgency of a cowboy trying to suck rattlesnake venom from his arm. I thought his ears might explode.

"A lot of people open accounts," I reasoned.

"Not everybody," Jeff said. "But that's not my point. Think about it. She could close it at any time. Why doesn't she?"

I didn't have an answer. "Maybe she doesn't read it," I hoped. "She never responds."

Jeff frowned. "Come on, dude, wake the eff up. You're in dreamland. Of course she reads it. She *likes* the attention."

I hadn't thought of it that way. "So you're saying—"

"I'm saying the fat ugly beast likes it."

His words bothered me, but I didn't challenge them. "No." I shook my head. "That can't be right."

Jeff slurped up the last of his shake. "I'm not saying it's right, I'm not saying it's wrong. Look at it from her point of view. She's a total loner. She's got no friends. So she opened an account and probably thought, like everybody else does, 'Hey, gee whiz, I'll see what people really think of me.'" He paused. "Now she's finding out."

"Do you ever think about *not* doing it?" I asked.

We were seated on benches at a small table. Castellano glanced out the window, his eyes following a pretty girl down the sidewalk. He didn't answer.

"Well?" I prodded.

"It's a goof," he said. "You don't have to be super mean. Write something funny. Don't worry so much, Sam. Laugh at it. Believe me, she loves it."

Deep down, I knew it was a lie. A lie we told ourselves to help us feel better. There was no way she liked that kind of ridicule. Nobody could. But that night, when I played my part, I repeated that lie to myself over and over until I almost believed it.

I tried to be as not-mean as possible, while still keeping my comment at acceptable levels of snark.

I saw you in the rain with your butt-ugly dog. Who was walking whom? Woof.

(Obviously, my heart wasn't in it.)

The next morning, I slid the card into Athena's locker and went directly to the nurse's office. She stuck a thermometer in my mouth and said there was a nasty stomach bug going around. "Yeah," I told the nurse, "that's probably it."

SOMEBODY LAUGHED

I don't think I can write in this journal anymore.

I don't want to.

Screw it.

But this is a promise I made to myself. I decided that—for Morgan, in her memory; for me, for today—I would unplug the world and let my thoughts leak out like a puddle of blood.

I can't stop these thoughts. I need a cork. But what happens next?

I implode?

Somebody laughed in the hallway today and it sounded like Morgan. I turned around, forgetting just for that sliver of a second. Hope filled my chest. And it was just some random girl, cackling over something.

Some days I hate everyone.
But no one more than I hate myself.

SORRY

I need . . .
I need . . .
I need . . .

something.

That's it for today, people, move along. Nothing to see here. Nothing at all.

THE GREAT AUK

Today Mrs. Dolan told us the story of the great auk, an animal that was basically the original penguin, more or less. A flightless bird. It went extinct in the 1800s.

The auks lived in isolation on an island off Iceland somewhere. They couldn't fly, so they just hung around, had babies, and that was life. Far from men and women.

Until one day, some sailors came along.

You have to imagine that for centuries, nobody ever bothered the auks. They were all set. I like to think that one of those big, dumb auks looked out at that first ship and thought, "Oh, goodie, here comes company. That's nice!"

Well, no, not exactly.

It was the beginning of the mass slaughter. Because those dudes in the boats, probably half-starved at that point, stared at all those strange birds and thought, "I wonder how they taste?"

So mankind came, killed, ate, left, came, killed, ate—like the island was the world's first fast-food restaurant. Easy targets.

"You want fries with that auk?"

Those auks, what chance did they ever have in this world?

THE WATER TOWER

I visited the water tower. By myself. There's a big fence there now, topped off with barbed wire, and a locked gate. It's like a prison that they are trying to keep us from escaping into, like there's something good up there. A safe place, like in the zombie show *The Walking Dead*. Which is pretty funny, if you ask me. A prison is where you go to escape the zombies.

Anyway, when a school kid commits suicide, the adults get busy, making it look like they TAKE THINGS SUPER SERIOUSLY. And they do, I'm sure. The fence was a sign of that. ("We're not taking this lying down, no siree!")

I got over the fence in less than a minute. Cut my hand, but not so bad. There is a high ladder along the side of the tower, with small round metal rungs. I climbed it rung by rung, just like Morgan must have done two months before. It took courage, I'll tell you.

Courage or, maybe, desperation?

Maybe not caring was the key to everything.

I was trying to figure it out. I wanted to become her, to feel it, to understand. All I knew was I needed to get up there, stand in her exact same spot.

I didn't know what to expect. I didn't even know why I wanted to get up there. *Wanted* isn't even the right word. I *needed* to stand there, precisely in that place, follow in her footsteps.

So up and up I rose, higher and higher. That's an old song, "Your love," blah, blah, blah, "has lifted me . . . HIGHER!"

And your cruelty, blah, blah, blah, brought me . . . crashing to the earth.

I stayed up there for a long time. Stood right at the edge too. Felt the breeze on my back, swayed a little, but I was never going to take that step.

I'm not like some people.

I have to think a long time before I do anything. So that's all I did up there. Think and blink, think and blink.

THE WATER TOWER AGAIN

Not so easy shaking the memory of yesterday.

No matter how hard I try, I can't imagine ever taking a step like that.

SORRY

It feels cold
in here,
doing my fifteen minutes
in solitary,
staring
at these bare white walls
like pages . . .

I forgot what I wanted to say.

ONE TRUTH

The truth?

Morgan and I were alone together 14 times. Exactly that. I've counted. I find myself revisiting those times at odd, unexpected moments. Waiting for sleep, eyes closed to the dark that surrounds me. Those are the visits I conjure myself, like Aladdin rubbing the lamp. What slays me is when I'll have sudden visions of her while mixing chemicals in science lab, or on the bus, groggy, staring at the window, listening to some random comic's podcast.

Like, for instance: I was eating a bowl of cereal after school. I'm shoveling it into my face, brainlessly watching television. And suddenly I imagine her sitting across the table from me. The table floats away. Our knees nearly touch. I don't know what makes me do it, or why, but I cup my two hands up to her face and she leans into them, sinks into my warm hands.

We don't speak. Though it feels to me—and this sounds so weird I can barely write it now—like she is purring. Somewhere deep in the cave of her chest, a satisfied animal rumble. It is as if I am a healer, and I gave her a momentary rest from all life's hurts and pains and betrayals. It was a spiritual thing, almost. I could feel her smooth skin on the tips of my fingers, in the hollow of my palms. The delicate cheekbones of her face. The weight of her head pressing into me. Her eyes are closed and relaxed. She is at peace.

I don't know if that ever happened. Did we even do that once?

Or did I just make it up now? All I know is, either way, it was real.

It feels real.

And that's all that matters.

THE BEAST

I didn't realize that I liked her. Or as Morgan might describe it, that I like-liked her. Not for a long time, anyway. I mean, she was okay. Not nearly as awful as everybody made her out to be. I didn't get that at all. Obviously there was something bad between Athena and Morgan, something nobody seemed to understand. How do you dissect a person's hate? Were we supposed to pull it apart, piece by piece, try to uncover the core of the problem? Nobody really thought about it much. We had our own homework to do.

A fierce hatred radiated off Athena like steam. I heard a phrase the other day, my mother was talking about an incident at the bank, and she said, "I was so angry I couldn't see straight." And I got it instantly. Full-on furious emotion, it's all you can see. That was Athena with Morgan. I don't think she saw Morgan as a real human being anymore. I can understand this now, months later, long after it is too late. To

Athena, and I guess to the rest of us, Morgan became a thing, an object moving through the halls of our school, occupying our seats, breathing our air.

Over time, that became true for most of us. We failed to see the person. She became this . . . beast. That's when the nickname started, I'm not even sure who came up with it. We called her "The Beast" or sometimes TFB or TUFB: "The Ugly Fat Beast."

Because we were so freaking creative.

Even though she wasn't fat, and she definitely wasn't ugly. Mostly we knew her as "Beastie."

(My bestie the beastie!)

Others called her slut.

I guess it made it easier to hate her.

THE SISTER

I saw her sister today. Very strange. It was one of those times when the halls were empty and I was late for class. I turned the corner and there she was, spinning the dial on her locker. She looked up and I knew it was her, Morgan's older sister, but I didn't want her to know that I knew.

Something like that.

You know, the dead girl's sister. That can't be easy.

I kept rolling down the hall.

She looked like Morgan, but prettier, I guess. Thinner, taller, hair lighter, more fussed over. Anybody could tell they were related, though, which must have been weird for her. Because it was definitely weird for me. So I motored past, but she called out, "Excuse me? Can you help?"

I'm like, "Huh?"

She smiled, embarrassed. "My locker is spazzing out on me. I think I'm doing the combination right, but it won't open. I'm, like, five minutes late already."

It was just us in the hall, so it wasn't like I could melt into the crowd or anything. If I could have evaporated right there, I would have. *Poof,* you know. Gone. Instead I said, "Yeah, they stick sometimes. You gotta kind of . . ."

I punched the top right corner of the locker with the side of my fist. *Boom.* A loud, echoing, rattling sound. Then I pulled up on the handle real hard and—*fliiiiiing!*—the door shivered open in my hand.

"Cool," she said. "Thanks."

"Sure," I said. "Any time."

There were a lot of thoughts racing through my head right then. About eighteen different things I could have said.

"I'm Sam," I told her, and added idiotically, "Sam I am," and scooted out of there fast.

DOUBTS

How do you say
sorry
& actually mean it?

DAD'S GUN

My father keeps a gun on the top shelf of his bedroom closet. Way in the back. He stores it in a wooden case that's lined with felt, like the inside of a fancy guitar case. There's a lock on it, but he never locks it. I guess Dad figures he doesn't want to be fumbling for the key when the zombie hordes smash through the windows.

(*Braiiiiiins, braiiiiins*!)

I discovered the gun a couple of years ago when I was searching for Christmas presents. I'm the kid who will check every corner of the house if I think there's something good hidden. I like poking around in people's secret places. Finding Christmas gifts is my specialty.

The first time I found it, the gun scared me. Now, not too much. The truth is, I never felt for one minute that I would actually use it on myself. I couldn't imagine ever feeling that way. But I tried to bring my mind to that place.

The despair, the hopelessness. I slumped against the closet floor and stared at the silver gun in my hand. A .38 Special Colt Diamondback. It was horribly beautiful, or beautifully horrible.

Time passed, no idea how long. The bullets were in the box. If I wanted to, it would have been so simple. In a momentary impulse, I could have pushed the barrel up against the roof of my mouth and squeezed the trigger.

Boom.

Lights out.

Crazy, right?

And it would be done. All over. I'd never get a chance to take it back. There would be no . . . oh, wait, hold on. Did Morgan actually understand that? Could her mind wrap around the finality of it? Maybe that's all she saw, the end of her suffering, the black, blank silence of the departed. No more bells, no more noises, no more voices and their terrible, disapproving faces. No past, no future, no more sad todays. No tomorrows.

I placed the .38 back in its case, returned the box to the shelf in precisely the same spot. My father would never know I'd held it in my hand. He'd never know what I thought about. Every kid has secrets. Parents are mostly in the dark.

SOMEBODY'S FINGERPRINT

This is going to sound dumb. Or lame. Or just really, really boring (so I'll keep it short). But I've been staring at my fingertips for the past ten minutes. I took a black marker and pressed my colored-in thumb onto a white page. There I am. That's me. Those bumps and contours, the ridges and lines. It looks like the topographical maps Mr. Haycox made us study in P.E.

(Which was annoying, by the way.)

In the old days, P.E. was this awesome thing where kids played dodgeball, climbed ropes, and smacked the hell out of each other. Now there are actual bubble tests and all this phony learning. It's not enough that we run around and sweat, now we have to dance and cooperate, play games of "Trust," and have meaningful activities. Shoot me now, you know? Anyhow, that's how I learned about topographical maps and backpacking, which is what I thought about after staring at my fingerprint for the past ten minutes.

The FBI can identify people by their fingerprints. We're all our own unique snowflake—isn't that corny? Nobody else is exactly like me. Which is amazing also, when you think about the world filled with more than seven billion people. I look at those bumps and lines and wonder how that could be possible? There's got to be some kid in Somalia or wherever with my exact fingerprint. The lines, the ridges, exactly the same. Identical.

I'm a little worried about how much I've been thinking about my fingerprints. All the places I've been, the things and people I've touched, the marks I've left behind.

SHE LIKED BATHS

She was the most random person I ever met. Everything she said surprised me. Her mind roamed around like a hungry animal, foraging for food.

"Do you take baths?" she asked.

"Almost never," I answered.

"A good hot bath can fix just about anything," she said. We were in the cemetery next to the school grounds. If that sounds creepy, it wasn't. The cemetery was actually a really pretty, peaceful place. And best of all, it was private. Morgan closed her eyes and stretched her arms. "I learned that from *The Bell Jar*. She took a lot of baths in that book."

I didn't understand most of what Morgan talked about. I felt like a moose staring dumbly over the rim of the Grand Canyon. It was amazing but . . . incomprehensible. Nothing organized itself in my mind. Words and ideas shifted around like sand.

She kept talking about baths, the relief of sinking into hot, hot water. The mirror all fogged up so you couldn't see yourself, even if you wanted to, which you didn't.

"I sometimes take two, three baths a day," she said. "But the water always gets cold, and then I feel like a slab in the morgue."

"What?"

"A cold pancake!" she chirped brightly, performing a sudden, graceful twirl, her arms outstretched, spinning like a snowflake in a storm.

I stood there, drawn to her like a magnet, understanding none of it, not a word.

A corpse in a morgue?

"There's nothing sadder than a cold pancake," I finally said.

She stopped spinning to stare at me, staggering a little, still dizzy from her whirling dance. "You're right!" she exclaimed. "Cold pancakes suck ass. Let's climb a tree!"

Then she raced off, giddy, toward the tall pines.

I followed. What else was I going to do? Like I just wrote, I was metal (mental?) and she was my magnet.

MEETING WITH LANEWAY

I scoped out his office a few times, strolled down the hallway, checking out what's what. One time the door was open and I spied Laneway at his desk. I half-stepped, half-leaned in, and said, "So this is where the magic happens, huh?"

He pulled on his mustache, closed the book on his desk. "Hello, Sam."

I glanced around the small, cramped office, bursting with books, boxes, piles of papers, articles and photographs torn from magazines and thumb-tacked to bulletin boards. "I see you're a hoarder," I joked.

He leaned back in his chair, hands hammocked behind his head, and looked around at the office as if seeing it for the first time. He said, "People usually ask me, 'Why do you keep all this stuff?' And I always wonder, 'Why do you throw it all away?' "

"That's one way of looking at it," I said.

He didn't say anything. Just looked at me, waiting.

"Well, anyway, just saying hi." I inched out of the room.

"Are you free?" he asked.

I hesitated. "I've got band."

"I could write a pass," he offered. "Sit, if you'd like."

So I sat.

"What's up?" he asked.

I looked down at the hands on my lap. "I started a journal, like you suggested."

"I'm glad to hear that, Sam. How's it going?"

"I'm trying to keep up with it," I said. "A little bit every day."

Another silence. Maybe Mr. Laneway couldn't think of anything worth saying. Maybe he didn't mind the quiet.

Finally, he asked, "Has it helped?"

"Helped?" I repeated. "You mean, like with . . ."

"Morgan," he said.

There were no windows in his office, and I really could have used a window right then. The air felt suddenly stagnant, the walls too close.

"I sometimes think it was my fault," I said, unbelievably. I mean, I never intended to say that to anyone.

He sat up a little straighter. "Is there a reason why you feel that way?"

"A reason? Like *one* reason? No," I said.

Then I talked for a while. Not about the message board, not that, in so many words. But maybe I gave him enough to figure it out. Mostly I talked about Morgan and me. The times we hung out. And how I rejected her at school. It was impossible to tell all of it. But bits and pieces came gushing out, like blood from a sliced thumb.

"And how are you feeling about all this?" he asked.

(Seriously?)

"Pretty crappy," I said.

"Yes," he replied. "Yes, Sam. I can see that. Let me ask you. Is this about her social media page?"

(He knew? He knew!)

I looked away from his serious, super-earnest face. All I could do was nod yes. "Some," I said.

"I see."

More silence, but a worse kind. This one was heavy, thick, sorrowful.

I studied the tile pattern of the floor.

"You participated in it?" he asked.

"I wrote some things," I said. "Then I stopped."

"Did you ever tell anyone?"

I shrugged helplessly.

"That must be a hard thing to live with," he said.

At first, I thought he meant Morgan. Because, obviously. Then I realized he was talking about me. I was the one who lived.

Mr. Laneway pushed a box of Kleenex toward me. I frowned, wiped my eyes with the back of my sleeve. He stood up, walked away, returned with a glass of water. "Thanks," I said, and drank it.

"In times like this," he said, now leaning against the front of his desk, close to me, voice very quiet. "In these times," he sighed, searching for words, "many good, decent people look within and find ourselves wanting. We can't help but wonder."

I wasn't sure what he meant, but the sound of his voice made me feel better.

"We ask ourselves, 'What could I have done?'" he said. "We feel—"

"Like failures," I said.

"Yes, like failures," he said. "But that's only natural. It probably means that you're a caring person."

"I don't know, doubtful." I shook my head. "I really don't."

"I do," he said. "When someone takes her own life, Sam, it's a horrible, awful, heartbreaking tragedy. We can never fully understand why."

I nodded, sniffled.

He said, "We can't know what goes on inside someone's head, or the circumstances of her life, or exactly why anyone does the things she does. Depression can be a devastating illness. We have to live with that unknowing."

I looked into Mr. Laneway's face. "My parents tell me that I have to move on, but they never told me how."

CLEAR ALL

We never touched.
We never kissed.

I never put my arm around her.
Never held her hand.

But we did text.

And on the day she died,
after I heard, I cleared

every message in my cell,
wiping away the prints.

I wish I had that day back.

I would remember, then,
not to forget.

GROUNDHOG LIFE

"You ever see the movie *Groundhog Day*?" Morgan asked.

"Um, not sure."

"You must have," she said, knocking me on the shoulder with the side of her fist. "Everybody has. Bill Murray is a weatherman who gets stuck in a time loop, where he has to live the same day over and over."

"Yeah, okay," I said, remembering. "I might have seen that."

"That's what my life feels like," she told me. "I go to bed, hoping that after a long sleep I'll feel better. But each day it's exactly the same. Nothing changes. I can't snap the streak."

"Maybe you need to try something new," I suggested.

She looked at me thoughtfully, in that way she had of looking at me. "You mean . . . something radical?"

"Maybe." I shrugged. "Go on a hot-air-balloon ride, learn

to play the banjo, take up painting, join the Y, go skydiving or something."

"Skydiving!" she said.

"I don't know, it's super expensive," I said. "How did he get out of the time loop in the movie?"

She paused, head tilted. "I don't remember," she said, smiling. "That's funny, I have no idea how he finally did it."

GOTTA GET GOING

I remember one afternoon—just an absolutely gorgeous post-card afternoon, the kind of day when troubles lift away—I was lazing in the cemetery with Morgan. She checked the time. "Oh shoot, oh crap, oh shoot!" she gasped, and got all panicky and flustered. "I gotta go, I gotta get going, I gotta go!"

"Huh, what?" I said helpfully.

"I gotta go, I'm late, oh shoot!" she said—and I saw that her hands became bees and her hair was tangled and her eyes were wide and wild and—

(She was crying.)

I didn't understand the sudden stress.

"What's happening?" I asked.

She snatched up her things—her phone, her bag, her cigarettes. (Morgan had started smoking, stealing cigarettes from her mother.)

"It's Wednesday. My father picks us up for dinner on Wednesdays at 5:00, and he's super strict about the time—"

I checked my cell. "It's, like, not even five now—"

"I still have to get home, dumbass!" she snapped.

(And I forgave her instantly, because she was obviously flustered to the maximum, as wigged as anybody I'd ever seen. And over what? A few minutes late? Her hands kept brushing and pulling and adjusting her clothes like crazed bumblebees.)

She sniped, "I can't, like, travel back in time, okay? I have to run home—and he's totally going to flip. I'm so dead," she sputtered.

"Wait, what?" I called in utter failure.

She ran and ran, and I sat there blinking.

SHE QUIT DANCE

Sometimes we texted.

Morgan: *I quit dance.*
Me: *Why? You love it.*
Morgan: *Doesn't matter.*
Me: *But. You. Love. It.*
Morgan: *It doesn't love me back.*
Me: *Okaaaaay.*
Morgan: *I feel relieved about it. Happy.*
Me: *Happy is good, I guess.*
Morgan: *Yes. It's all good.*

THAT TIME I KIND OF TRIED

I once tried to talk about it with Morgan. You know, that thing that hung over her neck like an ax. The trolls online.

I learned never to try that again.

It was tricky from the get-go, because I'm not good at talking about, ahem, *real things*. As a rule, I'd rather not. Also, I didn't want Morgan to know what I knew—or that I had been any part of the crapstorm on her social page. So I tried taking the long way around.

We were at a new place, for us. The playground behind her old elementary school. It was pretty sweet and absolutely empty. We sat up in an awesome pirate's ship like a pair of seaworthy scalliwags.

"I can't stand the way my teeth stick out," Morgan complained.

"I never noticed."

"I should have had braces when I was younger, but my parents . . ."

"You look fine," I said. "No one cares."

"When I get older, I'm definitely going for plastic surgery," she said.

"What the what?" I said. "Are you going to buy a big set of plastic boobs?"

"Maybe." She laughed. "Or a nose job, or a stronger chin. My lips are too thin. I look like a chicken."

"Can you buy false lips?" I asked.

"Botox," Morgan said. "Look at my face. I have a lazy left eye. My nose is sort of squished. And I have totally a white person's lips."

"You *are* totally a white person," I pointed out. "You need to stop, Morgan. You are fine the way you are."

(I know, I should have said "beautiful," but: *integrity*! Plus, I didn't want to send the wrong message.)

"Fine? That's it, huh?"

"You look like yourself," I said. "Like Morgan."

"That's the problem. I don't want to look like me," she said.

"Why are you suddenly so weird about yourself? Plastic surgery is gross."

"I don't think so." Morgan shrugged. "If you can improve what you've got, and you're rich, why not go for it?"

"But those Hollywood actors look so fake. It's ridiculous. They can't even smile," I said.

Morgan stood, stretched, and went over to the slide, where she zipped down surprisingly fast. "That thing's dangerous," she warned, right after I came down headfirst. We messed around on the swings for a few more minutes, rode the ceramic pelicans on springs, then shifted over to a bench beneath a shady maple tree. We were six years old all over again, missing only individual juice boxes and a Tupperware container of Goldfish crackers.

Morgan checked her cell and it instantly annoyed me. "Seriously, Morgan," I said. "Are you really looking at your phone again?"

"I really am, yes," she replied. "That's exactly what I'm doing."

"Maybe you could unplug every now and then," I suggested.

"Oh please, Mother. Are you going to talk at me today?" Morgan said. "Unplug? That's how they kill old people in hospitals."

"Seriously, Morgan. What's so great on there that you have to read it while I'm sitting here right next to you?"

She told me she was following the feed about some Disney celebrity who got arrested for drunk driving. Morgan claimed there were tons of embarrassing photos all over the internet. Everyone was slamming the celebrity on Twitter, nonstop one-liners. Morgan read a bunch to me out loud. At first the comments were clever, then cruel, and eventually just mean.

I said, "I sure hope she doesn't read all that stuff."

"What do you mean?"

"I wouldn't want to read it if it was about me," I said.

(See what I was doing there?)

"Look, Sam," Morgan answered. "She nearly ran over a baby in a stroller, then she bit the cop who arrested her. Dude's got to get tetanus shots! So I'm thinking she deserves whatever she gets."

"Yeah, but . . ."

(This wasn't going as well as I'd hoped.)

I tried again. "The trolls write such awful things. Look at the kids in our own school. Some of them say horrible things about people."

Morgan swiveled her head to look at me in a searching sort of way. "What are you talking about? This doesn't have anything to do with our school."

"Nothing, I don't know," I said.

"If I were some big celebrity, and people were talking about me, I'd want to know about it," Morgan said. "Burying your head in the sand isn't going to help."

"I don't agree. When you read those idiots, you disrespect yourself," I said, my voice rising.

She stared at me. "Wait a minute, Sam. Are you talking about me?"

She stood, hands on her hips.

"No," I said. "No, no. I mean just anybody."

"I think it's funny," she said. "Nobody takes any of that stuff seriously."

I didn't say anything, just sat there and felt depressed.

We were quiet for a minute. Morgan standing, scrolling through her phone, tapping away; me resisting the urge to throw it against a brick wall.

Finally, Morgan wondered, "Hey, Sam. Do you think my hair's too thin?"

SOMETHING

It wasn't a date, but I guess it was *something*.

Our secret something.

We decided to see a movie together. We were a boy and a girl, yes, but it wasn't *that*.

I'm not even sure how it came about. Oh yeah. One afternoon by the log (we had discovered the most perfect place to sit in the woods behind the elementary school and christened it cleverly "the log"), Morgan was really perky and she started talking about this thing she really wanted us to do. And I mean: really-really.

"I want to go to the movies with you and sneak in tons of food," she said. "It'll be hilarious. Huge foot-long sandwiches, bags of candy, chips, drinks. A total feast."

"How are we going to smuggle all that in?" I asked. "Excuse me, young man. Is that a foot-long sandwich in your pants, or are you just happy to see me?"

(*Ha,* she laughed. "Good one!")

"We should do it," Morgan urged.

"We should," I fired back before thinking.

"All right, let's," she decided.

Um . . .

"This Saturday," she said. "We'll go to the earliest show."

And I was like, "Sure!" before my brain caught up to my mouth and screamed: WHAT THE HELL ARE YOU DOING?

Too late.

This wasn't a date. To be clear.

But still! It was *something*. The idea of it felt different.

The movie couldn't have been more random. Morgan couldn't care less what we saw. This was her deal. She opted for a scary movie—*The Haunting* or *The Conjuring* or *The Corn* or whatever it was called, *Paranormal 16*!—at a theater on Elm Avenue, a long bike ride away. It was the easiest theater we could get to by ourselves, without involving parents and a million questions neither of us wanted to answer.

But also this: I felt it was going to be *our* time. No one to see us, no one to judge. We'd do it on our own. Forget the wicked old world for a few hours.

I worried.

"Don't worry," she said, reading my mind. "No one goes to movies at 10:30 in the morning."

And she was right, *and she was wrong*.

No one was there.

But I should have worried. Looking back, this was our

happiest, purest few hours together—and the beginning of the end. Within two days, she would hate me.

(I'm not ready to tell that part yet.)

First we pedaled to Marco's Deli. Again, totally Morgan's idea. She was the mastermind—and loaded with cash. "My treat," she said.

"No, no, no," I protested.

"Yes, yes, yes! I've got gobs of birthday money," she said. "Let me."

I looked at her, uncertain.

"Really," she insisted.

I ordered a turkey sub with bacon, because: bacon! Morgan wandered the aisles and returned clutching packages of gummy worms, chocolate, soda, chips, all kinds of junk.

"Breakfast of champions," I noted.

"I know what I'm doing," she said.

I picked out an Almond Joy bar from the candy display.

"Coconut is evil." She frowned.

"Right," I said, putting the candy bar back on the shelf. "What was I thinking?"

She stuffed everything into a huge cloth bag and slung the bulging sack around her neck.

"This will actually work?"

"They never check inside a girl's bag," she replied. "Trust me."

And I did trust her. We were good to go.

The theater was practically empty. Morgan was right about that too. We huddled in the last row, far-left corner.

A few stragglers filtered in, lonely types with uncombed hair and massive buckets of popcorn, nobody I recognized. After the previews, we brought out the feast. Sound the trumpets! We ate like the Knights of the Round Table. Morgan whispered all through the movie, comically commenting on everything that happened onscreen: "Don't go in there! Is she a moron? This actress sucks nugs. I would never leave that huge knife out on the counter—not a good idea, Sugarlips," and on and on.

("Sucks nugs" was a new one on me. "It's short for nuggets," Morgan kindly explained.)

We weren't rude. Morgan kept her voice quiet, like the way you might talk in a crowded elevator or library, and I had to lean in to hear. I felt loose strands of her hair tickle my face, smelled the warmth of her mint-flavored breath.

(We had just plowed through a box of Junior Mints.)

It was fun, I was happy, and she was happy too.

Then I said, "This is like our secret world, you know."

"Yeah," she answered.

"Nobody even knows we're friends," I said. "It's like we're in a bubble. Here's to our impossible friendship. No one ever has to know."

She didn't have anything to say. Morgan got like that sometimes. She'd go dark for stretches, like that space on the dial between radio signals. A few moments later, I heard the *clink-clink* of glass in her bag. She pulled out two little bottles of rum, like the ones they have on airplanes. I was pretty surprised.

"Pass me your soda," she said.

"What are you doing?"

Morgan emptied the bottles into my cardboard cup of Coke, stirred it with her pinky. She took a long sip, took another. "Here," she offered the cup to me.

I took a sip. It tasted gross. I faked it, real smooth. "Cool." I half-gagged and gave back the cup.

She recapped the empty bottles and returned them to the bag. "I've got a system," Morgan said. "I use these bad boys to steal booze from my parents."

"Don't they miss it?" I asked.

She shook her head. "I used to replace the booze with water, but," she shrugged, "my parents are basically clueless. Besides, my dad's not around much anymore. He's checked out. Cheers!" She took a long sip.

Later she emptied two more tiny bottles into a new cup of soda. I didn't drink any. It kind of freaked me out, to be honest. I never expected it from her.

"Baby," she teased. Her voice got louder as the movie wore on. She laughed more often. Her breath lost its minty freshness. Something sour took its place.

You know that feeling when you leave a dark theater and step into the sunlight? It only happens after matinees. There was a line of people outside buying tickets. I blinked away purple dots, blinded by the daylight. After my eyes adjusted, I saw Jeff Castellano staring at me. I'll never forget the look on his face. A combination of shock, sorrow, and disgust. He was standing in line with Gavin Flynn and Demarcus Alston.

I felt like I'd fallen into a well. I was alone in a deep, dark place.

I tucked my head and took off around the corner. "Hey, wait, the bikes are the other way, dork," Morgan called after me. I kept my eyes fixed on the ground and hurried as if my hair was on fire.

I kept berating myself, the same words echoing in my head: *What a mistake, what a stupid mistake!*

NOTHING

I refused to get our bikes until I was sure they had gone inside the theater. Morgan didn't understand any of it. "What's wrong with you?" she asked.

I pulled out my phone, stared at it. There was a text from Jeff: "WTF?"

"Nothing," I said. "Just chill please, okay? Is that too much to ask?"

"Fine." She shut her mouth, crossed her arms, and leaned against a brick wall. Already I could feel a distance separate us. She was five feet away, but that brick wall might as well have stood between us.

(Things can turn to crap so fast.)

Riding home in unhappy silence, she asked, "What did you mean before, about being in a bubble?"

Something in her voice put me on guard. "I don't know."

"You don't know?" she repeated. "You said it, but you don't know what you meant?"

I glanced in her direction. She was glowing with anger.

"I was happy, that's all," I said. "It felt like, I don't know, nobody else existed except for us."

"And what about our, um, what were your exact words? I'm trying to remember. Oh, I've got it: 'our impossible friendship,'" she said, her voice dripping with resentment.

I kept pedaling.

She continued, spitting out the words as she rode behind my right shoulder, like a devil (or an angel) in my ear. "It's impossible for us to be friends—or, I should say, for you to be friends with someone like me—because why?"

This would be over in ten minutes. Almost home, almost home. I had to keep pedaling, keep rolling forward.

"We are friends," I said.

"As long as no one else is around," she shot back.

"They saw us!" I nearly shouted. "How dense can you be?"

She pulled over and sat on the curb. I circled back, steadied myself with one foot on the ground without getting off.

"What are you talking about?" she asked. Her eyes looked distracted, moving from object to object, never settling on me. "I don't understand you."

"Jeff Castellano," I said. "He was at the movie theater with Demarcus and Gavin. They saw us."

"So? What did you think would happen?"

I groaned, shook my head. *(What a world, what a world.)* "Maybe it doesn't matter to you," I said. "But on Monday, in school, it's gonna suck to be me."

In that instant, I saw all the hurt and confusion drain from her face. It was replaced with something else, something cold and terrible. "Forget you." She rose to her feet, awkwardly yanked at the bicycle, stumbled, moved to ride away.

"Wait," I said.

"Why should I?" she said. "You're just like them."

I called after her, "I'm not. I'm not!"

I watched her pedal away. I didn't know it then, but I do today. She was right. I was just like the rest. I was afraid to be anybody else.

SATISFACTION GUARANTEED

She was the one
who killed herself.
So why do I feel
like something inside of me
died?
This makes no sense
at all. I may ask
for a refund,
weren't we all born
with guarantees—satisfaction
or our money back?

THE REFUSAL

Looking back now, I can see that I made a series of mistakes. I imagine them as a line of circus elephants, sad gray trunks clasping short tails.

Going to the movie with Morgan . . .

Getting *caught* with her . . .

I realize—I do, I really do—that the worst mistake was the first mistake, putting *anything* on her message board. I own it now. I should have never done that, and I will regret it forever. It was like rolling a snowball down Mount Everest. Eventually that one mistake became an avalanche.

(Does that even remotely make sense? How do avalanches work? Just another thing I don't know.)

My second-worst mistake was making the wrong enemy.

On the Tuesday after the movies, I got "tagged" again.

Let me back up. The timing could not have been worse.

I was in a sour mood already, annoyed by everything, pissed off at the world.

How can I describe it?

Everything got under my skin. The sound of people's squeaky sneakers in P.E., the idiocy of teachers and their pointless homework assignments, the noise in the hallways, morons shoving, girls jabbering, people yelling "squeeeee!" It was like I was living in a different universe. I felt alone and disconnected. No Wi-Fi.

That's when I opened my locker and learned that I'd been tagged.

No, I thought, *not today.*

I've had enough.

She's had enough.

I had to do something. I knew Athena would be at the lacrosse game after school, because her burly boyfriend, Fergus Tick, played on the team.

It was time to tell her what's what.

She was standing with a group of girls, chatting loudly, laughing, not paying much attention to the game. For once in my life, I wasn't nervous. I strode right up. "Can I talk to you?"

She looked at me like: *You? Really?*

My face must have answered back: *Yeah, really.* Because Athena shrugged and followed me as I walked out of earshot from the others.

I stopped and held out the card. "I won't do it anymore."

Athena didn't react. She showed no emotion. She just placidly looked at me for what seemed like a long moment.

Her skin, I noticed, was flawless, smooth as fresh-fallen snow. The old nervousness came back to me. I shifted on my feet, waiting uncomfortably. The card wavered in my hand between us, while she stood there deciding my fate.

I imagined that Athena was like one of those medical examiners on *CSI*, and I was the cadaver on the table for her inspection. Her eyes burned green, but without warmth. Still, she didn't quite know what to make of me.

Finally, Athena brought those perfect lips into a smile and showed two rows of dazzling white teeth. She plucked the card from my hand. "I'll fix it." She brought her hand tenderly to my face—her soft fingers smelled of vanilla wafers and cut lemons—and said, "No worries, Sam."

A sudden cheer rose up from the sidelines. Our team celebrated before the opponents' net. Sticks were raised in the air. "Athena! Fergus just scored!" Wendy cried.

Athena turned to watch the field, momentarily forgetting me.

Fergus let out some kind of howl from deep inside his belly. "Aaaaaaarrrrgggghhh!" He strutted and bumped chests with his teammates. Fergus, I figured, would probably make a good congressman some day.

Lacrosse looked like a rough game, where big guys whacked each other on the arms with sticks. I was glad I played baseball. "So we're good?" I finally said, after the on-field celebration died down.

"Sure, no worries," Athena said, caressing a hand across her tight abdomen, as if realizing that she was suddenly famished. I almost thanked her, but I'm glad I didn't. "Okay, then. Um, catch you later, I guess."

She inclined her head to her phone and sent a quick text, scrolled, read, beamed, sent another. I stood by, unsure if our conversation was over or not. Satisfied, Athena pocketed the phone and gave me a radiant smile, the way a gentle sun might gaze upon a small planet. I stood bathing in her luminous rays.

"Oh, Sam. I almost forgot to ask," she said, ever so warmly. "Have you seen any good movies lately?"

"Wh-what?" I stammered.

(WHAT?)

I think, in that moment, I might have gone temporarily blind. Everything a blur.

She knew.

Athena gave a queenly sweep of long, thin fingers. "And don't worry about that other thing, Sam. It's been handled."

HANDLED

Fragile.

Handle with care.

Do not fold or mutilate.

THE FALLOUT

I wrote before in this journal that we never touched. That wasn't strictly true.

It happened on the day after I spoke to Athena by the lacrosse field, between second and third period. The main hall was filled with shuffling hordes of students, moving like cows in a slaughterhouse. Morgan grabbed me on the arm.

I could see fury in her eyes. "You . . . two-faced . . . liar!" Her fists were clenched. No, her entire body was clenched. Morgan's blazing eyes looked wild, red-rimmed. I could see that she'd been crying. "I can't believe you were one of them all along."

"What?" I said. "I didn't—"

"Don't lie!" she shouted. "Don't even—"

It was literally as if she were unable to speak. Morgan's mouth opened and closed, opened and closed, but she could not find the words. It looked as if her entire operating system had failed. *File not found.* At last, Morgan raised her right hand and slapped me across the face. The blow made such a huge sound that everyone—and I mean everyone—stopped to stare.

Morgan turned and stormed away. She stomped toward the main doors. Huge drama.

"Miss, excuse me, miss?" an elderly hall monitor called after her. "Unless you have a pass, you can't—"

Morgan didn't turn around. She was nearly to the door.

I became intensely aware of the eyes and faces that surrounded me.

Eyes everywhere, all focused on me, then Morgan, then back to me. My friends, my classmates, kids I didn't even know. They were all watching to see what I'd do, wondering what it was I did.

(I knew what I had done, and knew that she knew. Instantly I realized that Athena had sent Morgan a text. She had handled things, all right. My secret was out. To the one person who mattered, I was not anonymous anymore. She finally saw the real me.)

"Dude, did you see that?" a voice whispered. "That girl whaled on him."

Another guy laughed.

I was an actor performing on a stage, in a play in which I wanted no part, but I recited my lines perfectly: "You. Fat. Ugly. Beast."

She heard me. No question. I made sure that everyone

heard me. More laughter now. The audience was back on my side. *Bravo, bravo!*

"Miss, oh miss?" the monitor kept calling.

(Who hires these people?)

The door flew open with a crash. Morgan had left the building.

IDENTITY

Sam I am.
I am
Sam.

I am, I am, I am.

HOURS SEEM LONG

"Sad hours seem long." William Shakespeare.

Don't get the wrong idea, it's not like I'm one of those deep guys who actually likes reading five-hundred-year-old plays with insane language. I didn't have a choice. In English, we read *Romeo and Juliet,* which is basically *West Side Story* without all the music, dancing, and greasy haircuts.

It made me think of Morgan a little bit. Not like we were ever a couple or anything, not like that at all. It was more the way we lived on separate islands floating in the same sea, like the Montagues and Capulets, or dogs and cats. It's an old story, I guess. I didn't see a way for us to be normal in school, freaked about what people might think.

School is only where we live about 35 hours a week, after all.

I had my friends, and she had whatever. Her mind? Her family? The little bottles of booze and cigarettes? Whatever other secrets she kept?

I guess.

Shakespeare called Romeo and Juliet "star-crossed lovers." Somehow nature itself was opposed to their ever getting together. It was against nature! So it ended the way it did—twin suicides, *bam,* back to back. Bring down the curtain.

That's why I hate school sometimes, and why I'm not too proud of myself either. At least Romeo and Juliet were courageous. They didn't care what anyone said. They followed their crazy, twisted, star-crossed hearts. The hell with everybody else.

What did I do? I'll tell you: I blinked and stood there and wondered what just happened. I guess that's still me today, except now I have a pen in my hand. I'm the guy with a journal. She is gone and I remain.

"Sad hours seem long."

GOOD DOG

Really, really glad
I have a dog right
now. Max gets me,
understands, has no use
for the internet. I wish
I could be that pure &
true. Glad to just
lay here, dear dog,
and love you.

LANEWAY, REVISITED

I began to see Mr. Laneway every two weeks. "Just to check in," he called it. We even ate lunch together a few times.

Once he told me this idea that I can't escape. I can still picture that moment with such clarity, the exact day of the week, what he was wearing, even the stupid Tweety Bird necktie he wore. I can even see the framed photograph on the wall behind his desk. The photo wasn't much, just two silhouetted figures on a beach with a caption that read: "*The first to apologize is the bravest. The first to forgive is the strongest.*" Typical Laneway. His office was filled with feel-good messages.

"I've been thinking, Sam, that maybe you've been getting bad advice." He smoothed the tie between his fingers. "At least we should explore that as a *possibility.* People say that you have to move on, put it behind you. But let's consider the opposite. Maybe, just maybe, you need to put it *in front* of you—look directly at it."

I felt an electrical jolt in my body, like a guitar's plucked string, *thrum, thrum, thrum.*

"I've tried," I said, "a little bit, in my journal."

"Well, that's good," he said. "You should keep at it."

"What's on the other side?" I asked.

He didn't understand.

"I mean, after I dig into it?" I asked. "Where do I come out when I finally get to the other side?"

The prospect scared me. I didn't want to confront that monster.

"I can't tell you that, Sam. I don't have the answers. I'm only here to help with the questions."

On the way out, I saw Athena seated on the bench outside Laneway's office. I didn't like seeing her there. This was my place. Her presence soured it. Even worse, it linked us again, Athena and me. I glared at her with all the anger in my heart. Athena's face went white—she shrank back, as if it were painful to withstand my gaze. Somehow she didn't look so amazing anymore. Mostly, she looked frightened.

That's the moment when I felt the most confusing sensation of all: I felt sympathy for the enemy.

BABY STEPS

Morgan finally answered one of my texts.

She said:

STOP TEXTING, DORKFACE.

Progress!

SPRING

She got worse in the spring
as if every flower,
and every new leaf,
was an insult.

SPIT AND SHAKE

Our friendship was never the same after that scene in school when Morgan slapped me in the face. But on rare times, perhaps because we were both lonely, both confused and full of regret, we formed some kind of truce.

Weeks passed. We still walked our dogs, found ourselves in the same place—almost as if by accident and not design.

On those days we stood together like a pair of mismatched socks. Like nothing had ever happened. Somehow the physics wasn't right, the way we stood in relation to each other. She pulled away, and I was more distant too. It was like in Earth Science, when two tectonic plates shift.

(Yes, a 73 on the last impossible exam, thanks a lot, Mr. Hoffnagger.)

We both had changed, I guess. Morgan's changes were more obvious. She wasn't the same girl anymore. It used to be that with me at least, she was more open. Now her guard was up. Our trust was gone.

Okay, I am trying to be honest in these pages. I didn't know what she was going to do. Nobody did. Otherwise, maybe I would have done things differently. I mean, I *know* I would have done things differently. I gave up when she needed exactly the opposite thing from me. When she pushed, I should have held on tighter, tried harder.

When spring came, baseball season kicked into gear. I was on the school team, playing travel and rec, plus taking hitting lessons at Frozen Ropes. It sucked up all my free time, but I was happy. Baseball's hard, for sure, but it's a lot easier than regular life. You get a hit, you make an out. You catch the ball or you drop the ball. It's all pretty straightforward. And I know this might sound stupid, but even the ball is perfect. Seriously. It's the perfect object. Bowling balls are too heavy, footballs are too weirdly shaped, golf balls are too small. Baseballs have a smooth white surface and eighty-six stitches sewn with red thread.

(Yes, I've counted. Kidding! I read that somewhere.)

A baseball is the perfect machine, built to be thrown and caught. Most guys, I'd rather have a game of catch with them than actually sit and listen to them talk. As long as there's a ball zipping between us, and we're standing on a field of green grass, I'm as calm as a cow.

Max wasn't too happy with me those days, since I didn't have time to give him proper walks—and when I did, it was short and quick. I began avoiding the field, steering clear of Morgan. One hot May night, those nights when it stays light long after supper, I took Max out for an exploration. We tramped through the woods behind the middle school, up through the cemetery (I know, I shouldn't bring my dog there . . . but anyway!).

Suddenly, Larry went crazy: *Bark-bark-bARK-barky -BARK!*

The hairball was glad to see me.

Morgan was sitting on the ground, her back up against a tree. There was no one else around. Just a girl hanging around under a tree, like an apple that had fallen to the ground.

"Hey," I said.

"S'up," she replied.

It was weird at first, but after a couple of minutes, we started talking a little. She seemed jittery and, I don't know, *off* somehow. Morgan told me she felt all hollowed out.

"Have you been sick?" I asked.

"No," she said. "Not like that. Never mind. I'm used to it. I've felt like this forever. Nothing changes."

I don't know, somehow it felt sad and uncomfortable to me. Spooky in a way. I didn't want to hang for long. "Look, it's getting dark. I should go," I said.

"You ever spit and shake?" she asked.

"What?"

"Spit and shake," she repeated. "You spit on your hand and shake."

She slurred her S's a little. I noticed a red cup a few feet away. It might have been litter, but I didn't think so.

"Spit and shake," she insisted. "Do you know it or not?"

"Like a swear?"

"Yes, a solemn promise."

"So, um, no, I never have," I said.

"If you tell me a secret, I'll tell you something . . ."

"Yeah, no," I said, shaking my head. Something about her creeped me out. "I'd rather not."

"Ssssure," she said. "It's jussst that, I was thinking that maybe I dessserve to feel this way. Maybe this is exactly how I should be feeling."

"What are you talking about, Morgan?"

"Nothing," she answered. "It doesn't matter."

I think she was trying to open a door that night. Did she want to let me inside? Maybe. And you know what? I didn't want to know. I just didn't.

I started to go. "Are you leaving?" I asked.

"No," she said, and after a few failed flicks, held a lighter to a cigarette.

"You shouldn't smoke, it'll kill you," I said.

She laughed. "I'll quit someday, jussst for you."

"Spit and shake on it?"

"Not today," she said, pointing a finger at my face. She took a deep drag and blew rings into the night air.

"You're seriously going to stay here by yourself?" I asked.

"Sure beats home," she said.

"School tomorrow," I reminded her.

"You know what? I never see lightning bugs anymore. You ever notice that?" Morgan asked.

"Not really," I said. "It's a summer thing, anyway."

"I remember chasing them when we were kids. We called

them living lights, rising like sssparks into the sky. My sissster and I would run and catch them. We kept them in jars with holes in the lids."

"Yeah?"

"I remember," she continued dreamily, "how I wanted to keep them so badly. My father was like, 'No, no, you have to let them go,' but once I hid the jar in my backyard under the bushes. The next day, I forgot all about them. I was a kid, you know?"

"Sure," I said.

She squeezed the fingers of her right hand, three times each finger from the base to the tip, a new nervous habit. "When I found the jar, weeks later, they were all dead. I killed every firefly."

"That's sad," I said.

"I know," she said. "I cried and cried. And my father got sooo mad."

I didn't know what to say.

It was like we were almost friends once, but we weren't anymore. Now she was just a weird girl, getting drunk and smoking cigarettes under a tree. She scared me, I guess.

"Let's go, Max," I said, and got out of there.

KNEW HER

"I knew her," I said. "We were friends."

Morgan's sister looked at me, uncomprehending.

I could be such a loser. Couldn't even make a sentence.

I said, "Your sister, Morgan. I knew her a little bit."

Sophie didn't take her hand off the button to the water fountain. The water continued its liquid arch into the porcelain sink and down the drain.

"Why are you telling me this?"

I shrugged helplessly. Looked away, stared into the fountain. "Are you going to—?" I said, gesturing at the water.

She caught herself, released the button, and the water stopped. She looked at me strangely, as if she were afraid of something I might do, or might *be*.

"I thought you should know," I said. "If you ever, you know, wanted to talk."

Her fingers automatically went to a ring on her right

hand. She twisted it, a thoughtless habit. I could almost hear Sophie swallow. A dry, parched gulp.

"Here," I said, pressing the chrome button to the fountain. "Take a drink. I'm buying today."

She nodded, as if from a great distance, dutifully bent and took a short sip of the clean, clear water. She held back a few loose strands of hair, keeping them from getting wet in the sink. I recognized the ring on her finger. I'd seen it before on Morgan.

Sophie rose up and wiped the water from her lips with the back of her hand. "Thanks," she said.

Three girls appeared beside us, curiosity in the latest fashion. They were probably wondering why Sophie was speaking with a skinny, ridiculous, younger boy. One said, "Sophie, are you coming? Mary J said she'd drive."

"In a minute," Sophie replied. "You go ahead. I'll catch up."

The girls gave a chorus of affirmations and left.

Sophie turned her focus back to me. "You helped me with my locker once. I remember now. What's your name again?"

I told her my name.

And without thinking, these words rose up from that same deep, dark well. "You must miss her," I said.

Sophie's mouth opened as if to speak. Her eyes flickered with something, a thought, a memory. The mouth closed. "I have to go," she decided. "My friends—"

"We could walk if you want," I offered.

"No, no. Not today," she said, and just like that, abruptly hurried away.

SUMMER MEETING

This is the last time I saw her, maybe.

I hadn't seen Morgan since school ended, almost eight weeks ago. I looked for her every once in a while, but a lot was going on in my life—summer vacation on the Cape, travel baseball, hanging out—and it wasn't like Morgan was my big priority. Life goes on, right? I never saw Morgan out with the dog, or even in front of her house the few times I pedaled past.

Then, one day, there she was.

She looked bad.

I murmured like a cartoon hypnotist, "You seem sleepy . . . verrry sleepy. Seriously, Morgan, you've got dark bags under your eyes."

She frowned. "Are you trying to tell me I'm ugly? I already know that."

"What? No, nothing like that. It's just that your eyes are bloodshot. You look exhausted."

"You sound like my sister," she replied.

I stood there with my foot in my mouth, chewing on the toes. There was no way to talk myself out of this awkwardness. Our friendship, or whatever it was, had ended. Now we had only this distance and regret. "I'm just saying," I bleated.

Her smile was wan—there was no other word for it—a wan smile. Lacking in energy or happiness. The mouth smiled crookedly, but her eyes said otherwise. "It's okay. I don't sleep much," she confessed.

I nodded, grateful for the opening. "About once a week, I'll crash hard. I'll go to bed super early on a random Wednesday. Next day, I'll feel great. Last Saturday, I slept until 12:15, a new personal best. You should try it sometime."

Her gaze followed the dogs as they sniffed their way toward the stream. A sparse forest of trees stood beyond that. I heard that kids partied in there, smoked, drank. To me, it wasn't a world I knew much about. Stories and rumors, that's all. Not my world. Even so, I smelled the odor of alcohol on Morgan's breath. I watched as she fished a cigarette out of her pocket and lit it with a disposable lighter. She inhaled deeply, let the smoke ease out of her nostrils.

"Is smoking a regular thing now?" I asked.

"I don't sleep," she said again, quietly and matter-of-factly.

"What do you do all night?" I asked.

She shrugged, bored with me. "Stuff. The internet."

"I have to sneak my phone into my room at night," I said. "My parents make me unplug at 9:00, unless they forget."

"I'd kill myself if my mother ever tried that," she said.

(I know, she really said that. I know.)

She yawned and really did look dead on her feet.

"Sounds drastic," I said.

"Yeah, no worries. My mom wouldn't dare take my internet away."

And that was it. The last time we talked. It's amazing how little we ever said, as if we didn't know the same language. She was a bird up in a tree, singing a mournful song. And I was just a dog, barking at the clouds.

THINGS SHE SAID

It's raining crazy hard today with fat drops like water balloons. The howling wind shifted and now the rain falls slantways, drumming against the windowpanes of my room, like sticky radio tunes I can't keep out of my head.

I love wild weather, big weather, when I can feel the awesomeness of nature and my own smallness in the face of it. We're all just nobodies, dancing specks of dust. Here and then gone.

(Not that I need to experience a tornado. *The Wizard of Oz* was enough; I'm good.)

Maybe it's the rain, but tonight I keep flashing back on things I remember Morgan saying. Small remarks, favorite expressions, random observations. It's weird how in books, a line that seems unimportant in the early chapters can grow in significance later on. So you remember the words in a new way, weighted with new meaning. The present keeps circling back on the past, the way Max will keep coming back to me on a trail in the woods, then race off to the next thing, then back again. That's how it's like now for me, thinking of Morgan. Everything that ever happened is filtered through the present, the things I know now: She's the girl I used to know who killed herself.

"I don't want to embarrass you," Morgan once told me. At that moment, she hit the nail on the head. I was embarrassed to be seen with her. That must have hurt her so much. But what Morgan didn't understand was that it said so much more about me than it did about her. My insecurity, my stupidity. If I felt better about myself, I could have stood beside Morgan as her friend. But instead I hid, afraid of what other people might think.

Every moment in our past has been trampled, tainted by what came after.

That's sad, a distortion of everything that ever happened between us. She's not just the dead girl. I can't let that be my memory of her.

Hey, Morgan. You were so much more when you were alive.

She complained, "I don't think I can stand another year of school."

(Wow, the wind is violent now. A big tree branch just fell on the neighbor's car! I hope the power doesn't go out. Wait, I'm going to find a flashlight just in case.)

Hold on.

(Back, whew: And it took forever! Did you notice? Carry on!)

She used to say how much she hated getting out of bed in the morning. Not a big deal, everybody says that. But there's a storm outside and I'm here in my room listening to music, remembering.

Another thing before I go: I'm also *not* remembering. Which freaks me out. She's slipping away. I forget more each day. Some details are hazy, the way she—

(Crap. Knew it! The lights just went out. Darkness.)

THE DAY I HEARD THE NEWS . . .

Life rolled on like a nursery rhyme.
Diddle-diddle, Fiddle-fo-fum. Ma's
tea kettle boiled and blew, the merry
mailman came, our black lab barked,
and the dish ran off with the spoon.
Nothing and everything changed.
I sat in my idiot room, still dis-
believing text messages of shock
and swoon. I powered off the phone.
Waited there on the edge of my bed,
feet pressed to the floor in fear
I'd otherwise float into space,
& just vanish too, like Morgan.
I stared at my dumb white hands,
the tips of my awful fingers, thinking
only this: *Useless. Useless. Useless.*

THE GIFT

It came in the mail about two weeks after she died. A tattered paperback. Well worn, as if it had been read a few times, folded, mangled, left in the rain. Corners of the pages had been turned down. On the inside front cover, I read her name in black marker: MORGAN MALLEN.

My heart was in my chest, the usual spot, but it felt like it had swollen to twice its size. Bloated, belly up, like a sick fish. I felt unable to breathe, stuffed with crap, a closet too jammed with junk.

(Sorry, I suck, can't describe this feeling. Is anyone ever happy with their words?)

I was afraid to turn the pages. Would there be a note for me? Some message for my eyes only? Flipping through the first few pages, I didn't find anything. It was just a book in an envelope, addressed to me.

Morgan had talked about it before. And I think—now that I can think, now that my brain has awakened—it's possible that she wanted to give it to me in person. She hinted about it, how I should "definitely" read *The Bell Jar* someday. Morgan said that it was as if the author, Sylvia Plath, had somehow peered deep into Morgan's own soul. She quoted the book once, as far as I know.

We were talking things over in our usual spot, on the log in the woods. This was back when we were still friends, before she found out that I was one of the trolls on her web page. Morgan was unhappy that afternoon, and sat there like a bump, wishing it were not so. She said, "If you expect nothing from anybody, you're never disappointed."

I thought those were such sad words. "You can't look at life that way."

Morgan kind of shrugged. "I didn't make it up. Sylvia Plath wrote it in *The Bell Jar*."

"Great, remind me not to read it," I said.

She looked at me for a moment, as if a bird had landed on my head.

"What?" I asked.

"Nothing," she said. "Just . . . nothing."

And now the book had found its way into my hands. How was that possible? Was regular mail that slow? She must have mailed it more than two weeks ago. It couldn't have taken that long to reach me. A mystery.

I studied the front cover, and the back. *Not yet*, I thought, *I can't.* I didn't dare. I didn't want to know.

But Morgan wanted me to have it, her gift to me, from one world to another.

I started to read.

DAD SAYS

My dad shrugs, says:
"Sometimes
You zig, other times
You zag."

Point being, my dad says:
"We all stand one day
On the crossroads,
and we have to decide
About this life."

I get it now:
With each action
I create my new
Self.

Get ready.
Because tomorrow I'm gonna zag
(just when you thought
I was going to zig).

PUBLIC SPEAKING

It was a big deal in school this year. Talking, talking, talking. We had to work on speaking in public—and we were graded on it too.

Most of the talks were dumb, some weren't. On rare days, kids actually said things worth hearing. I secretly admired that.

The courage.

On this day I was stressed that I'd be too nervous to speak. That I'd be sweating, stammering, unable to look anyone in the face.

But I was fine.

Better than fine. It felt good. For the first time since all this happened.

Sure, I was anxious before the speech. All day in school I felt tense, jittery. I was there and not there. Until the moment when I opened my mouth, I wasn't sure if I'd have the guts to go through with it. I didn't know how I'd say it. I just had to trust the words would come out okay, that I'd make sense. That maybe somebody would understand. Or not. Who knows.

Maybe I wasn't saying it for my peers in the classroom anyway. I was saying it for myself—my sense of self—and for her.

First period dragged into second period, then third, and fourth, and on through the day. Time marches like a good soldier, stiff-legged, chin up, a weapon on its shoulder. Finally it was time for me to stand up, speak out.

I had an 800-pound gorilla to get off my chest.

I began:

"My name is Sam Proctor. You guys know that already. I'm standing here in front of you, looking at your faces. You can see me, and I can see you."

Their faces were puzzled, borderline bored. I was losing them already.

"On the internet . . . ," I said, and momentarily the power of speech halted within me. I saw that one or two pairs of ears had perked up. Everybody liked the Internet. Paula Ligouri's face turned pale, as if she sensed something in the air. Like she sensed where I was going with this.

I tried it again. "On the internet, you don't have to show your face. You don't have to give your name. And you can be as mean as you want to be . . ."

FACE MEETS FIST

In retrospect, I don't think getting punched in the face was that bad. I kind of liked it. I mean, I'm not *recommending* it. "Oh yes, you simply must try the Punch-in-the-Face, it's divine. Far superior to the Knee-to-the-Groin and half the calories!"

Fact: Fergus Tick went *blam* and I went *boom*. Hitting the ground was worse than the punch—no disrespect to Fergus, who packs a wallop, but that concrete was hard.

To my surprise, I did not see stars. Pretty little birdies did not circle my head, chirping tunelessly. None of the typical things I expected after a lifetime's education watching Loony Tunes cartoons. I got hit, I fell, and my coconut throbbed but didn't crack. That was it. Fergus's fist caught me on the right cheek below the eye—Fergus was a lefty, who knew! Maybe a tougher kid staggers back but keeps standing. Not me. I flopped like a spineless jellyfish.

One punch and done.

Message received, loud and clear.

Surprisingly: Fergus was the one who looked frightened, and so did Athena, who stood watching. My confession in speech class shook them up. I had broken the code of silence. I said out loud what I had done to Morgan Mallen. I spoke the unspeakable. I owned the thing that nobody else wanted. And even though I didn't point fingers at anyone else, I could see that it scared Athena to the core.

She didn't look so pretty from my viewpoint on the ground. She looked like she'd just swallowed a poisoned apple. There was something evil in her soul, and she was rotting from the inside out.

The fallout after Morgan's suicide had not been a good experience for Athena Luikin. She'd become damaged goods, like an expensive glass vase dropped to the ground. If Morgan was the dead girl, Athena was the one we blamed. At first, Athena put on a brave face, the tough girl who didn't give a hoot. Over time, cracks appeared. Everyone knew Athena was the one most responsible for harassing Morgan. In a way, she fell victim to her own game. Athena was tagged too. Her tag read: BULLY. One by one, Athena's friends faded into the background until she stood virtually alone, if not for the unwavering loyalty of Fergus Tick.

Rumors went around that Athena was transferring to a private school in another town. "Good," we said. One morning, a FOR SALE sign appeared on her front lawn. There was talk of a lawsuit, damages and courtrooms. The reign of the queen was over.

So there I sat on the ground, head going *boom-ba-boom, ba-boom, ba-boom, fuzzzzzz.*

"Get up," Fergus demanded.

(So you can punch me again? I don't think so.)

"Leave him," Athena said. "Come on. Let's go, Fergus."

And go they did.

I waited for my head to clear. It wasn't so awful. It felt like waking up any school morning, that torturous distance between head-on-the-pillow and feet-on-the-floor.

I needed a hot shower. Or maybe a long hot bath. Morgan once said, "Baths make everything better." It was time to find out if she was right.

Despite all that, deep down, I felt fantastic. Like a million bucks. Terrific, awesome, happy.

(How weird was that?)

I wasn't on the wrong side of life anymore. I was now an enemy of the bad guys—and it felt great. I tasted something sweet in my mouth, a new flavor, but I couldn't figure out what it was until I spat.

Oh, blood.

I KNOCKED

I decided to do it. I had to.

I stood at her front door yesterday.

I breathed in and out, in and out.

Steady as a willow in a hurricane.

And I knocked.

Bark, BARK, barkbarkBARKbark!

I'd forgotten about Larry. The lunatic mop.

I suddenly, fiercely, insanely wished I had a mint. I breathed into my open palm. Yuck, gross. How was my hair? What was I doing here?

Time passed.

And the door creaked open.

The mother was standing there, wheezing slightly, sizing me up. The expression on her face said, *What now, dear Lord, what now?*

THINGS I LIKE

This is a list of random things I like.

I like baseball games that last extra innings. "Free baseball," we call it. I like weekends without homework, watching my little sister sleep with her puffy lips and the saliva dribbling out of the corner of her mouth. I like my bed made with the blankets folded down nice and perfect, just right. I like the cold, numb feeling of a package of frozen peas on my swollen face. I like the last bell of the school day and the sound in the hallways of a hundred lockers slamming joyously shut and the big hum of let's get outta here, let's go. I like funny videos with absurd cats (I realize it's a big joke to some people, but I do). I like memories of old vacations, camping trips and card games and nickel antes. I like the stars in the sky when the night is warm and silent. I like the sound of a swing and a miss on the baseball diamond, the absence of sound followed by a fastball popping into the catcher's leather glove, the *whoosh*-and-*pop* combo. I like that feeling when you see a girl and think, wow, that's all, just WOW, and you know you have to find a way to stand next to that girl somewhere, somehow. I like a brand-new box of my favorite cereal, when I know it was bought just for me. I like turning on the radio and a great song comes on that same instant. I like laughter, and promises kept, and friendly waves across open fields. I even like Morgan's lunatic dog that *barkbarkbARKed* with the soul of wolf.

I like being alive, and today I am, right now, saying yes to life. Yes, yes, and yes.

WORDS

Larry pounced on my shoes, *barkbarkbARKing!*

"You remember me, don't you, Larry?" I said.

"And you are?" the mother asked.

I didn't have a good answer. And in fact, I never expected to see the mom. That wasn't my plan. Yet here she was, a fairly gigantic woman in a huge floral housedress. She might have weighed three hundred pounds. She smelled of butterscotch and a scent that reminded me of Morgan, the faint whisper of booze.

She eyed me suspiciously, the door only half-open, ready to slam shut.

(I am Sam, Sam I am.)

All I had to do was open my mouth. It's all anybody ever wanted me to do, my parents, Mr. Laneway, Morgan. "Just talk," they said. "It's easy. Try it. Say one word. Start with your name . . ."

Seriously?

What good would that do? My name is . . .

Use.

Less.

Ness.

READING

Morgan had marked up *The Bell Jar* here and there, little checkmarks and passages underlined.

I never found my name in it. There was no secret message. Believe me, I looked.

"I shut my eyes and all the world drops dead" was underlined in red.

There was a loopy star next to "I wanted to be where nobody I knew could ever come."

(Oh, Morgan.)

Another star: "I had nothing to look forward to."

It was that kind of book, and I guess Morgan was that kind of girl. There was a sadness inside her, a darkness I couldn't touch. Strange as it seems, all the while I imagined her reading those words, dragging her pen under important sentences, drawing stars in the margins.

Reading is the most alone thing in the world.

But she was with me the whole time.

Weirdness. The book brought us closer, across time and impossible distance. We shared this.

YOU ARE

"And you are . . . ?"

I stood rooted before the door. My mouth twitched.

"And you are . . . ?"

She wanted me to identify myself. I was tempted to say, "I don't really know anymore." But what I said was:

"Hi, I went to school with your daughter—"

"Sophie? She's up—" the mother said, momentarily confused. Then her face changed, she heard it, *went to school,* the past tense. A shadow fell over the mother's distrustful gaze. She steadied herself with a hand on the doorjamb.

I stood watching her, not knowing where else to look.

"Come in," she said, not smiling. "And you are?" she asked again.

"Sam," I said, for lack of a better answer.

(Guilty as charged.)

I wished that I could peel the skin off my fingers. *Here, take my prints, analyze what I've done, and you tell me.*

Sophie appeared behind the mother, standing a few stairs above the ground floor.

"Sam?"

She looked good, shorts and a T-shirt. Sophie had no idea why I was there. Or, I don't know. Sophie was pretty smart. Maybe she knew all along.

"Hi," I replied.

THE APOLOGY

After opening the door, the mother returned to a large upholstered chair in the front room. She sank heavily into it, facing a large television set, a dish of hard candy by her side, a basket of knitting by her swollen feet. Music trilled, some kind of opera. She never again looked at me.

She scooped up Larry into her lap and with a thick finger scratched the dog's ear.

It was all a little weird.

Sophie said something to the mother that I didn't catch, and led me to a small back room she called the den. The room had dark paneling and drawn blinds, sunlight filtered through in dusty streaks. It smelled musty. We sat on the couch, facing an old TV that looked like it didn't work.

Sophie seemed out of place inside her own home. I wondered if that's how Morgan felt, like a stranger passing through.

"I'm shocked you're here," Sophie said.

"I know, I should have called. I'm sorry, I'm an idiot," I explained accurately. "Should I leave? This was a bad idea, wasn't it? I should leave."

I began to rise. Sophie placed a hand on my thigh. *Stay,* it told me.

I sat back, looking around. It was not a happy room, absent of art, photographs, even books.

"So," she broke the silence. "Why did you come?"

"I needed to talk," I said, "about Morgan."

She swallowed and her shoulders stiffened, as if preparing for a blow. "Okay."

"Remember I said to you that day, about how if you ever needed to talk? What I realized later on was that I wasn't doing it for you," I said. "I was doing it for me. You're the only person I know who knew her."

Sophie's fingers went to her ring, squeezing it, *squeezing it,* making sure it was still there. I couldn't read her face, didn't know what she was thinking.

"We were friends, I think, but the truth is that I was not a good friend to her," I began.

"You don't have to—"

"No," I interrupted, "I think I do."

And I told Sophie the entire story, all of it.

To her credit, Sophie listened to every word, the good times and the cruelties. All the while she sat quietly, hands folded on her lap, legs crossed, uncrossed, crossed again, a stricken look on her face. I noticed that as I spoke, she leaned farther and farther away from me. It felt like an invisible force field rose up between us, and I was Doctor Doom.

I don't know if I finished or just ran out of gas, like a car on a lonely road. "I came here to apologize," I said. "I needed to tell you that I'm sorry."

I looked to her face, hoping for mercy.

Sophie stood, rising with the exaggerated care of an invalid. She turned her back to me, spoke to the wall. "Is that what this was all about? You're here to ask for forgiveness? Will that make you feel better?"

"I'm not . . . *asking* . . . for anything," I said.

She turned and snorted contemptuously. "Can your apology bring my sister back?"

Her voice grew bitter, vengeful.

"I don't *accept*, Sam," she continued. "Do you understand? I don't accept your weak-ass apology. It's not good enough. It's not okay. It will *never, ever* be okay."

I sat in defeat, my palms open. All words failed me. Another horrible mistake. Wherever I went, whatever I did, I only made things worse.

I found I had nothing, nothing at all, to say.

"I need you to leave now," Sophie said. Her tone was calm, controlled, but ice-cold. "And Sam," she added, "I don't ever, ever want to see your face again."

OH WHY

She liked to sing. Have I mentioned that yet? Not that she had a good voice. But when Morgan sang, she did it joyfully and hysterically. Like any bird on a branch, Morgan was happiest with a song in her throat.

I like to remember her that way, singing loudly and badly in the cemetery—to the sky, the clouds, the gathering stars. She sang the hits on the radio, the crappy Disney stuff, rap, anything that caught her ear. But the song she loved the most was "Somewhere Over the Rainbow," you know, from *The Wizard of Oz.* Listening to her, I gradually got the words. *Troubles melt like lemon drops.*

I loved the ending, especially that pause in the last line, "Why—oh why—can't I?"

It was just an ordinary song until I heard Morgan sing it. That's when I first heard the ache in her throat.

WHERE DREAMS COME TRUE

And she will find
peace, and she will . . .
Forgive us.

I HATE THE WORLD

Falling, fallen, fell.

More than words
can ever tell.

THE ONLY ONE

A week after Sophie told me that she never wanted to see me again, she stood waiting by the main entrance of the school, like a vulture on a tree limb.

I tried to swing wide to avoid her, but Sophie stepped in my path. "Come with me," she said.

"Where?"

"Away from here." She started down the steps, away from the school.

I hesitated. "Wait, but school—"

"You're going to be late this morning. It's not the end of the world. The office doesn't start calling home until ten, so as long as we check in before that, nobody will know," Sophie replied. "Besides, you owe me."

The last stragglers entered the building. The doors closed. "Where are we going?"

"The coffee shop."

"That's five blocks . . . " I began to protest. She wasn't hearing me.

We walked in silence. Her pace was purposeful, all business. Sophie stared straight ahead, and I followed like a sad puppy. Inside the café, she exchanged greetings with the curly-haired guy at the counter. "Hey, girl. Shouldn't you be in school?" he asked.

"Fire drill," Sophie said. She ordered a complicated coffee. Asked me, "You want anything?"

I patted empty pockets. "I don't have any money."

"Figures. I've got it," she said.

The guy at the counter looked me over, not impressed. Eight thirty and he was bored out of his mind already.

(I could hear my father, "Go to college, kids.")

"Okay, um, I'll take a hot chocolate, please."

"Size?"

"What? Oh, um, small's fine. Tall, whatever."

"Whipped cream?"

"Yeah, yes."

We took seats at a table in the lounge area, which was sort of a fake living room deal—for that homey feeling—which was empty except for a few coffee-clutching types staring at their flickering laptops and cell phones.

Sophie sipped her coffee. "I never drank the stuff until I started working here part-time, nights, weekends," she explained. "Once you get hooked on coffee, it's impossible to wake up without it."

I tasted my hot chocolate. It was pretty awesome. I didn't get the appeal of coffee. Said nothing.

With a flick of her finger across her nose, Sophie signaled for me to wipe whipped cream off my face.

(Sigh. I'm a clown.)

"I've been thinking about your visit to my house," she said. "I appreciate that you were trying to do something . . . ," Sophie paused and surprisingly offered up a crooked smile. "Something . . . *noble* . . . the other day."

She cast her eyes downward, drawing her lips into a line, as if regretting the smile.

The expression, those downcast eyes, gave her a familiar quality. Then it hit me. I'd seen that same expression on her sister's face.

"I hated you," she said quietly. "I'm still angry. At you, at those cowards on the internet, at my parents, at the world, at Morgan . . ." She reached for the cardboard coffee cup. "That day you came over, I was like, '*Oh, poor you.*' Give me a break. You think you're the only one?"

"No, I don't—" I shook my head helplessly.

"I did crappy things too," Sophie said. "I wasn't there for Morgan, not like I should have been. I feel guilty too. So you don't win first prize, okay? You have to get in line."

"I never meant to—" I sputtered.

"Who do I have to apologize to? You?" she said. "My parents? There's only one person who matters, and she's not here."

A woman looked over at us, obviously trying to

eavesdrop, probably looking for new characters for her crummy, unfinished novel. She looked away when I gave her the devil's eyeball.

"She told me about you," Sophie said, lowering her voice. "Do you even know that? I knew about you long before that day at my locker."

"Wait, what? You knew me?"

"We were sisters," Sophie said, as if the bond of blood explained everything. "Maybe not the closest sisters in the world, but there were times, late at night, when we talked."

I sat back, trying to absorb this new information. Morgan and Sophie talking together, sharing secrets. "What did she say about me?"

"She liked you," Sophie replied. "She said you were a good egg."

"A good egg?"

(What the hell? An egg?)

Sophie shrugged. "Those were her words. She said you were one of the only people on the planet who treated her normal."

"I wasn't always nice. I did some bad things."

"No, you weren't perfect. Sometimes you were a creep, like a lot of guys," she said, but without malice. Sophie's eyes flickered with kindness, and she leaned forward. "And sometimes you weren't, okay? Morgan tried to kill herself before, more than a year ago, back over spring break. She took pills, drank. I found her asleep on the bathroom floor, called nine-one-one. They pumped her stomach at Roosevelt Hospital. I guess she never told you about that?"

I was stunned, nearly speechless. "I didn't even know her back then."

Sophie raised an eyebrow, gave a faint smile. "See what I'm saying. This is bigger than you. *Nobody* knew. My parents were ashamed, especially my father. He really freaked. They decided to keep it a secret. Morgan went back to school one week later, and we all acted like nothing happened. It worked for a while."

We sipped the dregs of our drinks in silence. Mine had gone cold. I checked the time on my cell. "Look, we should—I've got a math test third period."

Sophie didn't move. She wasn't finished with me yet. "You asked me to forgive you. I don't even know what that *looks* like, okay? I mean, it's not all right, what you did. But you weren't half as bad as some of the others. And I will *not* forget. Forgive and forget? I don't think so. Forgive and remember, that's your best hope." She paused, scratched a fingernail at the side of her coffee cup.

I waited. It was a trick I had learned from Mr. Laneway. He would sit like a turtle, careful not to fill space with empty words. He always allowed room for me to speak. Gave me *time* to find my thoughts and put them into words.

She now tore at the top edge of the coffee cup. "I am not strong enough to forgive you or anybody. Not yet. But I hope to be someday. For myself, not for you. I don't want my sister's death to define who I am."

"Mr. Laneway, this counselor at school—" I began.

"Yeah, I know him," Sophie said.

"He says forgiveness is the gift you give to yourself."

Sophie chuckled, rolled her eyes. "Words," she muttered. "I really don't think Morgan did it because of you. Her issues ran deeper than Sam Proctor."

A thought struck me. "I wondered about the book *The Bell Jar*. I got it in the mail like two weeks after—I never understood how that was possible."

The right corner of Sophie's mouth lifted. She really did have the same cockeyed smile. "Maybe you're not so dumb after all. I was the one who mailed it," she admitted. "In her note, Morgan asked me to."

IN THE STAIRWELL

A week later, I was late for class. I was charging up the back staircase three steps at a time and nearly ran over Athena Luikin.

She was alone on the landing between two levels, leaning against the railing. "Whoa, sorry," I said, before I even realized it was her. The fallen queen.

I took another leap, then paused. I turned back to look at her.

Athena's face was splotchy, her eyes swollen. Maybe it was because I stood higher on the stairs, but she looked smaller to me. Just a girl.

Fragile and alone.

And in tears.

"You okay?" I asked.

She shook her head. No, she wasn't.

There was justice in that. And a part of me was glad to see her suffer. Athena Luikin *deserved* to suffer.

I returned down the stairs, step by step, slowly, reluctantly, until I stood directly before her. There was something I had to know. "Why?" I asked.

She looked up at me, frightened. Unsure what I was going to do.

"Why did you do it?" I asked. "Why did you hate her so much?"

Athena took a step back, pressed into the corner of the railing. There was nowhere to run. We were alone in an empty stairwell of the school. Just us and, somewhere small and hidden, the truth.

"I can't go out there," she confessed. "I can't go to another class."

She didn't have to tell me why. "I heard you were moving," I said.

Athena sniffled, nodded. "Not soon enough."

"I need to understand what happened between you two," I said.

Athena looked away, as if scanning the wall for a secret passage through which she could escape. "We used to be friends," she began. "Isn't that bizarre? It feels like so long ago. We met in preschool. I invited Morgan to my birthday parties. We had sleepovers on Friday nights. We signed up for dance classes together. A couple of years ago, I liked a boy," she said, stifling a miserable laugh. "It doesn't matter who. I was obsessed over him. My first crush, you know? Morgan knew how I felt. I told her everything. But that didn't stop her. He was mine. Mine. And then one day, I found out she'd been secretly hooking up with him. Kissing him, and letting him . . ." She trembled, a cold quiver. To my eyes she said, "It was a slutty thing to do."

A boy. All this pain and loss over some dumb guy.

"That was the beginning?" I asked.

"And the end," Athena said. "We never spoke again." A new fierceness entered in her eyes, the old anger coming back. "I hated Morgan for what she did. She was my best friend. I never forgave her. Never."

"And now," I said, "no one forgives you. Funny how that works."

I turned my back and walked away.

At the top landing, I fired one last shot across the bow. "Better wipe your face, Athena. You look like hell."

THE NOTE

One afternoon, I naturally fell in stride with Sophie and walked her home, like any two friends after school.

"Was there a note?"

A long silence, because it hurt to speak.

I had asked a terrible question that led Sophie to an awful place. It didn't matter how much time passed. No wonder why she preferred to ignore me. It hovered over us like a gray sky full of dark clouds, threatening rain.

"Yes," Sophie finally said.

I wanted answers. "And?"

"It's private," Sophie answered. There was finality in her voice; a door closing. She did not look at me, but instead fixed her eyes on some distant something over the horizon. Two birds, the leafy branches of a tree, and maybe, ever-present in her mind's eye, the water tower.

I waited. I had to know.

Sophie said, "Morgan wrote a lot of things, actually. Some of it was really, really sweet—"

I could hear the catch in her throat, the hesitation, and her fierce refusal to cry. She wasn't going to give in to that, not here, not in front of me. I placed my hand on her back, felt her slight shudder at my touch.

"That note will be ours forever," Sophie said.

I walked beside her in silence, because sometimes there really is nothing to say. Just being there has to be enough.

I didn't dare ask if Morgan had written anything about me. I guess I'll never know.

JEWELRY STORE

I knew I couldn't do it alone. What did I know about what girls liked? So out of the blue, I asked Sophie for help.

She was suspicious when I told her what I wanted to do.

"And you want my help? I don't get it," she said.

"There's nothing to get," I said.

"It's a little weird," she replied.

"But not creepy, you don't think?" I asked, suddenly doubtful. That inner voice starting up again: *Idiot, idiot, idiot.*

"No, no. Not creepy," she said. "It's kind of sweet, actually. Okay, I'll do it."

"I don't even know where to go," I admitted.

"Well, what were you thinking?" Sophie asked.

I shrugged.

I wasn't sure that thinking had much to do with anything. It was more of a *feeling* thing.

That afternoon, we met outside Eileen's Jewelers at a strip mall not far from school. I had $40 in my pocket.

"Are you ready?" she said.

There was something formal about the way she asked me. I couldn't put my finger on it. But there was a new distance between us.

"Yeah," I said. "If you are."

Sophie pushed open the door. She led me to a glass case in the back. "Here are the bracelets."

A saleswoman with pointy glasses and frosted hair smiled at us. "May I help you?"

I shifted my eyes sideways at Sophie helplessly.

Sophie said, "Yes, we'd like to look at these bracelets." She pointed out a few. "This one, this one, and this one, please."

The woman took out the tiniest key I had ever seen in my life to open the glass cabinet. She set the bracelets out on a black cloth. Sophie laid them across her wrist so I could see better. I shrugged. "I don't know," I murmured.

"May I ask, are you two celebrating an anniversary?" the saleswoman asked. "You make such a cute couple."

"What? No," I said. "It's not for her. It's for . . ."

"I'm here as his advisor," Sophie said, offering a tight smile to the saleswoman. "You know how boys are."

"Yeah, I'm pretty clueless," I said.

No one disagreed.

Something in the case caught Sophie's eye. She bent low and pointed. "May we see this one? The amethyst."

The saleswoman brought it out. I immediately knew it was the perfect one.

That's when Sophie stepped back. "No, no," she said,

shaking her head. "I can't do this, Sam. I'm sorry, I can't." She turned and walked out of the store without another word.

"Sorry," I said to the saleswoman. "I think, let me . . . I'll be back. I hope."

I followed Sophie out the door.

She stood on the sidewalk with her back against the brick building. Her head was tilted up, eyes closed, face to the sun.

"Sophie, I didn't . . . ," I began to say.

She looked at me. "What the hell, Sam? What are you doing in there?"

I didn't exactly know. "I think," I finally said, "I'm trying to find some way to say I'm sorry."

Sophie shivered, shook her head, and looked away. "And you think a bracelet is going to get it done?"

"No," I said, suddenly angry. I felt the emotion rising up in me, and I didn't care anymore what she felt or thought. "It was a mistake, okay. I shouldn't have ever asked you. It was just another stupid, idiotic mistake! It's how I roll."

Sophie laughed. She actually let out a guffaw, right there on the street. "It's how you roll?" she repeated, smiling despite herself.

The tension between us was broken. "Yeah, I screw up all the time," I said. "I never do the right thing. But I'm trying, Sophie, I really am trying."

After a few minutes, we stepped back inside. The saleswoman hadn't moved, perhaps she had watched us through the large front window.

"Sorry," I said sheepishly.

"It's fine," she said. "You'd be surprised how often it happens." With a delicate hand, she slid the silver bracelet with the blue stone forward on the counter. The amethyst.

Sophie turned over the price tag. $56. "I think she would have liked this one, Sam. Amethyst was her favorite."

I felt like such a loser. "Maybe something less expensive? I only have forty bucks."

Sophie exchanged looks with the saleswoman. An unspoken language I did not understand.

"Well, let me see what we can do," the saleswoman said. "We just concluded a spring sale. I'll speak to my manager. Maybe we can knock off twenty percent."

"Twenty percent?" I said, trying to figure the math in my head.

"Twenty percent would be great, thank you," Sophie quickly said. And to me: "I can make up the difference."

"Are you sure?"

She smiled crookedly, and I glimpsed again the girl who fell from the sky. My friend, Morgan. "I would like to, Sam. If that's okay?"

Later, we stood outside, under a maple on the corner. I had a wrapped box in my hand. It was a warm afternoon. The sun beat down on our heads.

Sophie pushed back a strand of hair. "Thank you," she said. "That was hard, but it meant a lot, being here."

I held up the box. "Well, you were awesome. I couldn't have done it without you."

"What can I say? I'm half princess, I like shopping." She grinned. "But I'm curious, Sam. What exactly are you going to do with it?"

I shrugged. "It's complicated."

We stood there for another minute, looking at each other. I didn't know whether to hug Sophie or shake her hand or what.

So I hugged her. And for the first time in my life, it wasn't clumsy or stupid or awkward. It felt right.

We'd made it through another day, together.

THE LAST TIME I SAW MORGAN

I don't expect anyone to believe this. But I will set it down here, plain and true. As simply as I can say it.

Telling paper.

One late afternoon, I walked one last time to the water tower. The light was fading. I entered from the woods. No one was around.

Up I climbed, up and up to the top.

I stood, again, exactly where I imagined that she had stood.

Before she fell.

I closed my eyes.

Felt her presence.

And she was there.

A vision before me.

Her face, her body, floating in air.

"Hey," I said.

Hey, she answered.

"Is that you?"

None other, my brother, she said.

(A grin? Really?)

"Are you real?"

Real as you, she said.

"I didn't expect to see—"

Shhh, she whispered.

Her finger pressed against my lips.

It felt cold.

I shivered.

"There's so much I never said," I told her.

It's all right, she said. I know.

"I didn't understand what you were going to—" I said.

(My eyes grew warm, liquid.)

Don't, she said.

"I'm so, so sorry," I told her.

Not your fault, she said. You were kind.

"No. I wasn't," I said.

You were, she said.

We laughed.

(We did.)

You tried, she said.

"I failed."

You tried, she repeated. You cared.

"I still care."

Yes, you do, she said. I can see that, even from here.

"You should never have—"

Shhh, she hushed.

"But—"

I got worn out, she said. I made a choice.

"A bad one," I said.

She said she was sorry.

"Are you okay?" I asked.

(No answer.)

"Are you?" I repeated.

She smiled, ever so faintly, a whisper of sadness in her eyes.

"You should have stayed," I said.

Her shoulders lifted ever so slightly, fell again. A shrug, resigned.

I never loved anyone, she said. Ever. Please make that your gift to me.

"What?"

Love someone. Live long and love someone with all your heart, she told me.

"I will, I will," I promised.

Thank you, she said.

"Thank you," I answered.

(A pause, a wave, and gone again. Oblivion, painlessness, death.)

I stared wild-eyed into the trembling sky, at the ground below, at the leaves whispering in the trees. I felt like I was in a mystical place, touched by magic. She was fading from sight. And I knew this twilight was our last.

"Don't leave," I said.

No reply.

(Gone, gone, gone.)

My head dropped, my body shivered in the echo of our brief meeting.

I thought of Romeo and Juliet. How he raced to meet her in death. "Never was a story of more woe . . ."

It was not a move I'd make.

She was real. It was real. And I would remember, always, the cold touch of her finger on my lips.

Dusk now, now darkness.

Night fell fast.

Then: what's this?

A firefly appeared, and another, and another. A sudden miracle of fireflies in the night sky, floating lights flashing bright, and gone, and burning again in the silent dark.

I had to shake my head and smile.

Afterward, I gathered up what little was left of the scattered shrine, almost nothing. I left the bracelet for her, for the wind and rain and the eternal night to steal away, and bowed my head, and disappeared.

KINDER

Today Mr. Laneway asked me how I was doing and it turned out that I was okay, and I told him so. I think I was more surprised to say it than he was to hear it.

He suggested that I should consider taking an elective next year for creative writing.

I was like, "Really?"

He said, "You bet."

Problem is I'd have to miss lunch. That's my favorite part of the school day, the only time you can relax a little. When you give up lunch to take an elective, you have to grab snacks while you're walking down the halls. I've seen those people, the lunch-missers, and they are scuttering around like squirrels munching on nuts. Hyper-achievers. That didn't seem like me.

At the same time: Cool, Mr. Laneway likes my writing. I've showed him bits and pieces of my journal. Not everything, but some of it.

He says I have talent.

"More than talent," he said, "you have heart. It shows in your writing."

My jaw hit the floor. I probably stood there, shoulders forward and arms dangling, Neanderthal-like. Grunted, "Ugh?"

Maybe I'll do it. Maybe it is me after all.

This year I've learned to like writing, liking the person I become when I write.

The feeling I got was more important than what I actually (really-really) wrote.

Right here—on the blank white page—I'm beginning to see the real me. Does that sound like I think I'm all that? Because I so don't. But I do think that writing things down has helped me see what I really feel. Does that even make sense?

(Doubts, uncertainties. Carry on!)

It's hard to describe, but I don't know what I think until I read my words on the page. I read them back and sometimes I'm like, "Whoa, dude's pissed."

I might keep going with the writing thing. Who knows? Try to read more, think more—and by that I mean think more of *my own* thoughts, not a bunch of ideas borrowed from everybody else. My own shit, good or bad.

I grew up thinking that deep down inside me there waited the real boy, huddled in a corner. And if I just chip-chip-chipped away at it, it would be finally revealed: the true me. Like a sculpture made from stone.

Now I think the opposite might be true. We create ourselves out of nothingness, we are flesh and blood only. Sticks and stones and raspberry jam. The real boy is the person I create through my actions. My deeds and my words. The choices I make.

I am Sam.
Sam I am.

The real me is what I do, how I treat you . . .
And you . . .
          And you . . .

Um. I'll have to puzzle this one out another day. Getting fuzzy, brain's a little scrambled today (like eggs), and there's a zombie apocalypse on television calling my name.

I'm saying only this:

I'll be kinder
Tomorrow.

MR. SMOOTHIE

I'm just about at the end of this journal, a few more pages to go. I'll buy a new one soon and start fresh. But before I close this book, bury it in my dresser, I've got a couple more things to say.

I bumped into Athena at the mall.

Let me say it up front, I'm not a mall guy. My basic policy is, I'd rather not. So if I'm there, it's usually because I got dragged by my mother, or to catch a movie at the Cine 18 with some friends. But if I do go, it's mandatory that I stop for a mango shake at Mr. Smoothie in the food court. I'm addicted to that liquid.

I was with Demarcus and Jeff. We were seated around a table, our trays knocking around like bumper cars. Those guys snarfed burritos. I was happy with my awesome, extra-large mango shake.

Then D said, "Look, there's Athena Luiken. I haven't

seen her since she left school last month. She cut her hair wicked short."

I turned and there she was, sitting on the other side of the food court. She looked different now, paler, thinner, more fragile.

D snorted. "She probably joined the witness protection program. Athena doesn't exist anymore."

It shook me up, sitting there listening to the bogus hum of their voices. As if they knew anything. It all came rushing back. All the old feelings, images of Morgan, and my anger. After a few numb minutes, my heart contracting like a fist, I saw that Athena and her mother had gathered up their packages and were preparing to leave.

"Hold on a sec," I told Jeff and D. I stood with my tray in hand.

"Where you going?" Demarcus asked.

"I'll be right back," I explained, not really explaining at all.

I bypassed the nearest trash can, sailed through a sea of tables, and drifted into Athena's path.

Even at that moment, I didn't know what I would say, or if I'd even say anything. I was tempted to turn away, not acknowledge her. Why was I even waiting here? What was it D said? *Athena doesn't exist anymore.*

I stood there watching, waiting, holding the stupid tray as if it were a sacrificial offering. They came closer, walking side by side. The ghost who used to be Athena listened as her mother talked.

That's when Athena's eyes glanced in my direction. I saw her see me. Something terrible crossed her face, like a dark wind crossing over tall grass. It was a look I'd seen many times before on Morgan's face as she walked down the hallways of school.

Right at that moment, I knew Athena wished she could disappear. Maybe in the same way that Morgan had wished she could disappear.

What did I want from her, after all this time?

I didn't know.

I still don't think I'll ever understand it.

I remembered all those times in school when I looked up and Morgan was suddenly there. How I'd always look away. How I never said a word. How I failed her.

And now here came Athena Luikin, a shopping bag pressed against her chest, her head down, shoulders hunched, trying to appear invisible.

I remembered *The Bell Jar*. "I shut my eyes and all the world drops dead" was a line that Morgan had underlined in red.

"Hi," I said.

The word came out dry and brittle, like a dead leaf crumbled in someone's hand.

Athena looked up, startled. She almost smiled, nodded once, and kept walking.

She didn't apologize.

I didn't expect her to.

After all, neither did I.

I see you.

It wasn't forgiveness exactly, but it was the best I could do.

ONE LAST THING

I had one last thing to do.

I went to Morgan's page online. It was still up, a forgotten site in cyberspace, like a dusty attic in a big house.

I sent an e-mail to the host, explained things as best I could, and requested they shut it down. I scrolled to the beginning and read all the way through. Every anonymous comment.

No one was responsible, yet our fingerprints stained every word.

Die, die, die.

No one cares.

Fat ugly beast.

I opened a new comment box and wrote:

You did not die.

I still see your passing light

In the fireflies
That flicker and fade
Outside my window
In the invincible summer night.
I guess I will remember
Everything.

—your friend, Sam Proctor

Thank you for reading this Feiwel and Friends book.

The Friends who made

THE FALL

possible are:

JEAN FEIWEL, Publisher

LIZ SZABLA, Editor in Chief

RICH DEAS, Senior Creative Director

HOLLY WEST, Associate Editor

DAVE BARRETT, Executive Managing Editor

NICOLE LIEBOWITZ MOULAISON, Senior Production Manager

ANNA ROBERTO, Associate Editor

CHRISTINE BARCELLONA, Associate Editor

EMILY SETTLE, Administrative Assistant

ANNA POON, Editorial Assistant

Follow us on Facebook or visit us online at mackids.com.

OUR BOOKS ARE FRIENDS FOR LIFE.